THE MUFFIN MAN

A MODERN M/M FAIRY TALE

KIM FIELDING

Tin Box
— PRESS —

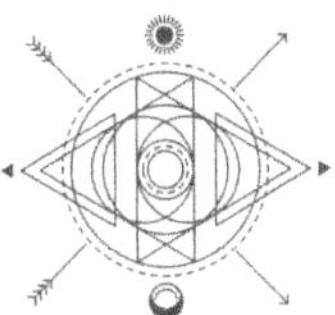

1

S *weatmonth, Year 26 of King Aurvid IV*
Udrodian Royal Palace

THE BREAD WASN'T QUITE perfect. Oh, it was good—almost everything Morli baked was tasty. But this time he was working with a sack of mysterious grains acquired from a trader who claimed they were from a kingdom far to the north. And because the grains were special, Morli thought the loaves should be special too. He'd used expensive thirst-flower honey as a sweetener, hoping it would set off the nuttiness of the grains. Yet as he chewed, he decided that the honey wasn't quite right. It was too... ethereal. These grains called for something earthier.

Hmm. Apple juice might work, but last year's apples were gone and it was too early for this year's. But what about catberries? Hadn't he seen a basket of them just behind the—

"Your Highness."

Morli turned around slowly, annoyance and dread swirling in his stomach, to face the stern-looking assistant chamberlain. "I'm baking," Morli said, although it wasn't exactly true.

"Their Majesties wish to see you. Immediately."

Both of them. Oh, demons' doorknobs, that meant trouble. "Let me just get my dough rising, and then—"

"Immediately, sir."

Morli untied his apron and hung it on a nearby hook, then gave his hands a cursory wipe with a damp towel. He was wearing an old tunic and hose, which was hardly appropriate attire for a royal audience, but *immediately* meant there was no time to change. He hoped they wouldn't scold him over his clothing too.

Fretting silently, Morli followed the assistant chamberlain out of the kitchens, up two flights of the narrow servants' staircase, through a series of small rooms, and then down a long hallway hung with faded tapestries. Demons' *doorknobs*—they were heading for the Blue Cabinet, which meant Morli would face his parents without an audience. That was never good news.

When he entered the room, he realized the situation was even worse than he'd feared. Under the cobalt-hued ceiling, standing among the desks and chairs and chests, were not just his mother and father, but also his oldest brother, Prince Algar. The assistant chamberlain exited and shut the door, leaving Morli to the mercies of his family.

"Your Majesties," he said to his parents, executing a creditable bow. Then to his brother, "Your Grace."

"Enough with that." The queen waved her hand impatiently. Sometimes Morli could pacify the king with exceptionally proper court etiquette, but his mother was never impressed. And now she scowled at him. "You have something on your cheek."

Automatically, he swiped at it. "Flour, ma'am. I'm sorry. I was told you wanted to see me right away, and I didn't have time to—"

"Yes. Because of course you were in the kitchens again."

In a perfect world, Morli would have taken that opening to explain that he'd just obtained a sack of intriguing exotic grains, and that if he experimented just a little more, he believed he'd find the perfect combination of ingredients and techniques to create delicious bread beyond anyone's imagination—the types of loaves poets would write sonnets about, if they wrote sonnets about bread. Which they didn't as far as he knew, but they should, because what in the entire world was more wonderful than a loaf still warm from the oven, crunchy on the outside and soft within?

Anyway, it wasn't a perfect world. His parents wore twin expressions of disapproval, while Algar, who stood slightly behind them, was making the same face as when they were boys and he was about to push Morli down a flight of stairs and then tell everyone that Morli had tripped.

So Morli simply nodded. "Yes, ma'am."

The king grunted. "A waste. A scandal and a waste. We have servants to prepare our food. That is what servants are for. You are a prince of the Kingdom of Udrodia, not a scullery boy!"

Morli had heard this lecture before. He'd tried to explain that baking was a noble and honorable pursuit. That as pursuits went, it was at least as worthy as the hunting and dice-playing and drinking that occupied the time of the middle two princes. That everyone in the castle enjoyed his food, including the king and queen themselves, and that when royalty from other kingdoms came to visit, they always exclaimed over the quality of the baked goods. But those arguments had previously gone nowhere, so now he gritted his teeth and said nothing.

The queen walked closer, her skirts rustling commandingly. She wore so many layers that it was difficult for her to sit. Rumor was that it took two hours for her chambermaids to dress her and another two for them to get her ready for bed, and that didn't count any changes of outfits she engaged in during the day. Morli thought baking was much more useful than spending the bulk of one's day putting clothes on and taking them off, but he wasn't going to say that. He valued his head too much.

"Morli," the queen said, her lips curled in a rare smile, "we have an undertaking for you. If you are successful, you will more than make up for years of disappointing us. Disappointing our subjects."

"I don't think most of the kingdom cares what I do. They have other things to worry about." He'd seen how people lived outside the royal palace, and he was certain that keeping their families housed, fed, and in decent health were much bigger concerns than how royalty spent their time.

"I care what you do!" she bellowed. The king nodded vigorously; Algar sneered. "This family has ruled for over seven hundred years, a dynasty few kingdoms can match. Seven hundred years from now, our descendants will still rule, and when they view our portraits in the Hall of Ancestors, they will look upon us with pride. They will *not* make jokes about the prince with flour on his cheek!"

"No jokes about the spit-boy prince," Algar chimed in, both inaccurately and unnecessarily. The king and queen ignored him.

Sorrow bowed Morli's shoulders. He'd known his

parents would never be proud of him the way they were of his brothers, who were good at shooting things or making snooty quips while standing around in fancy attire. But it hurt that they held him in such contempt. He was *good* at baking. Why couldn't that be enough?

"What is it you want me to do, ma'am?" he asked quietly.

She made a triumphant noise and gestured at the king, who strode to her side. He was always well turned out, famous for wearing clothing of burgundy velvet with extensive gold embroidery. He had a servant who did nothing but keep his lush gray beard in order. As a young man, the king had been a hero in a minor skirmish he liked to call a war, and shortly after his homecoming, his older brother, Vazam, had died from an allergic reaction to clams. Everyone had known that shellfish could be fatal for Vazam, and the cook who'd prepared his dinner that night swore he hadn't used any seafood in the stew. But the cook had been beheaded for his carelessness, and Morli's father had become heir and, a few years later, king. He'd married his second cousin and they promptly produced four sons which, palace gossips liked to whisper, were rather more than needed to ensure the continuance of the line.

The king stroked his beard. "You have heard, I assume, of the plight of Princess Osenne of Vraelum."

Everyone had heard of her misfortune. For years it had been the talk of all the kingdoms in the region, among nobility and commoners alike. Bards sang songs about it. Puppeteers put on shows in village squares.

Years earlier, the king and queen of Vraelum had insulted a sorcerer—a foolish thing to do, but also unfortunately easy. Sorcerers tended to have thin skin. This one placed a curse on the family, and when the princess reached her sixteenth birthday, she fell under an enchantment.

Sources differed as to the means of the enchantment—a spindle, an apple, a mirror, an imp—but everyone agreed on the result. Poor Osenne ended up imprisoned in a tower surrounded by an impenetrable bramble. Her parents had promised her hand in marriage and an enormous fortune to anyone who rescued her, but everyone who tried ended up impaled on the thorns.

Oh no.

Morli took a step back. "I don't want to marry Princess Osenne, and we don't need a fortune. We're wealthy already."

The king shook his head. "That is not the point. Additional income is always good, of course, and an alliance through marriage with Vraelum would be welcome despite your personal tastes, but—"

"You can always have sex with men on the side," Algar pointed out. "As long as Osenne pops out an heir or two, nobody will care who you sleep with."

The queen shot Algar a fierce glare and he cowered a little, which was gratifying to observe. But then the king continued. "But irrespective of the money and the political advantage, your quest will serve the greater good of bettering your reputation. The youngest prince of Udrodia will be known as a hero, and not as a... a...."

"A pot boy," Algar said.

"B-but what if I die?"

The king raised a finger and boomed out his response. "Some show their valor in life, and some become champions in death!"

THERE WERE ARGUMENTS. There was begging. There were even, to Morli's shame, some tears. But in the end it became clear that a dead gallant prince was preferable to a live baking prince, and he was sent on his way with a sword, an elderly horse, some packs of supplies, and a gloomy squire named Hendry.

"I'm not going anywhere near that bramble," Hendry announced when they were less than half an hour from the palace. "I'll follow you to the vicinity, but I'm not getting in reach of those thorns. No way."

Morli, who was walking because he wasn't sure the aged horse could handle a rider's weight, scrutinized Hendry. The squire's uniform was food-stained and too tight, his hair uncombed, and he looked at least as old as Morli, who was twenty-three. "Shouldn't you be a knight by now?"

Hendry scowled.

It took them a week to reach the outskirts of Vraelum. They stayed at an inn only two nights en route, which meant that Morli spent the rest of them consuming stale bread and sleeping in a bedroll while being eaten alive by insects. Hendry made terrible company and an even worse cook. It was a very long trip.

But it wasn't long enough for Morli's tastes, because on the seventh day they emerged from a thick forest into a vast grassland, where far ahead rose a lofty structure almost entirely obscured by a tangle of green and brown. Large dark birds circled above it. "Bet that's the tower," said Hendry, who wasn't especially bright and had a habit of stating the obvious.

Over the past week, Morli had more than once considered abandoning the quest. But his options were poor. He'd been told in no uncertain terms that he wouldn't be permitted back in Udrodia without a rescued princess and a sizable reward. He could have absconded to another kingdom—they'd passed through one on the way—but none of them would have granted residency to a cowardly prince. Maybe he could have taken on a false identity and found work somewhere. Bakers were always needed. But Hendry was there to rat him out, and Morli had no doubt the squire would do so.

Now he gazed across at the tower and felt very much like he was going to be sick.

"Maybe we should stay the night here. That way we can tackle the tower in the morning when we're fresh."

"*You* can tackle the tower, you mean. And it's not even midday."

True enough, and procrastinating wasn't going to make the problem go away. The dread was so awful that maybe it was better to just get it over with. "Fine," Morli sighed.

He began to trudge ahead but stopped when he realized Hendry and the horse weren't following. "We're staying here," Hendry said firmly.

"The tower's well over a league away. The thorns can't reach this far."

"Which is why we're staying here." The horse snorted as if in agreement and began to graze.

Well, fine. It wasn't as if Hendry was going to be helpful anyway. Morli made sure his sword belt was secure around his hips, gave Hendry a final baleful look, and started toward the tower.

The sun was bright and hot, and Morli soon wished he'd thought to bring a waterskin with him. His feet hurt. The king and queen had insisted he wear fancy clothing, and although his tall black boots were very pretty—Hendry was, at least, good at keeping them shined—they gave him blisters. Morli felt encumbered not only by his heavy sword but also with sadness that his family had sent him to this fate.

Worst of all, though, were the emptiness and regret deep in his heart. Despite his parents' oft-stated desire to marry him off to someone with favorable political ties, Morli had hoped to fall in love. He'd dreamed about it, imagining all kinds of scenarios in which he met a kind, interesting man who found Morli agreeable. Who wouldn't mind sitting in a kitchen, keeping Morli company while he baked. Who'd enjoy quiet evenings by the fire with a book. Who was smart and funny and didn't care about pomp or wealth. Who was even, Morli dared to hope, good in bed. He'd never found that man, and Morli's position as a prince meant he almost certainly never would. He hadn't even attained any true friends, let alone a long-term lover. But he'd dreamed nonetheless.

Was love so much to ask for?

By the time the tower loomed over him, the bramble so close that its green-and-wood scent made him sneeze, he was almost relieved. Maybe it was better to die young and fast than to spend a long life alone.

The birds he'd seen from afar were ravens. They perched on branches and on the jutting stones of the tower walls, rasping at him. It sounded as if they were warning him, but if so, their contribution was unnecessary. Rag-covered corpses—once young, vital women and men—hung among the twisting vines of the briar. They had been perhaps desperate to seize their only chance of wealth, perhaps impelled by visions of adulation for their courage, or perhaps, like Morli, forced by others. Now they were nothing but skeletons with trailers creeping through their ribcages and skulls, empty eye sockets staring sightlessly. Morli had never seen anything so sad.

Even while knowing it would be useless, he circled the bramble, looking for a way in. It took him over five minutes to make a complete circuit, but he didn't see even a tiny gap in the tangled vegetation. It was like no plant he'd seen before, bearing thorns as small as grains of sand or as long as his forearm, every one of them wickedly sharp. The dark green leaves were rough and spiny, the size of his hands; as far as he could tell, the plant bore no flowers or fruit. When he tentatively touched the vines, they swayed toward him like snakes. He hopped back with a startled meep.

Although the bramble obscured the lower half of the tower, there were windows above the vines. Morli cupped his hands around his mouth and shouted, "Hey! Princess Osenne! Are you there?" But no matter how loud he called, he received no response—which perhaps made sense since she lay locked in an enchanted sleep. Or maybe the princess wasn't even there. What if the entire story was a fabrication, and in reality Princess Osenne had eloped with a tinker and run off to another kingdom to live in happy obscurity? Morli wouldn't blame her for that. Worse, what if she had withered and died inside the tower? After all, it had been many years. Awake or asleep, how could someone go a decade without sustenance?

"This is stupid," Morli told the nearest raven. It croaked back at him. He thought it looked sympathetic, although it was hard to tell. "I don't want to do this. I wish my family accepted me for who I am, or that I'd had the courage to run away long ago." He sighed. "And I don't want to die. Princess Osenne's parents have an entire army at their disposal. They have sorcerers who might be able to block the enchantment. Why aren't they doing anything to help her?"

The raven didn't answer.

It occurred to Morli that perhaps Osenne didn't get

along with her parents any better than he got along with his. They might be perfectly content that she was locked up. He was fairly certain his family wouldn't lift a finger to help if he'd been enchanted. His parents would breathe sighs of relief that he was no longer embarrassing them, Algar would make jokes about it, and his other brothers would barely notice between their hunting excursions and their parties.

Morli sighed again. "I guess if Princess Osenne really is in there, that's pretty awful for her. I suppose I have to at least try to help." And he unsheathed his blade.

He'd been taking lessons in swordsmanship since he was five, and he actually wasn't half bad. He'd developed skills out of self-defense, because otherwise his brothers would have killed him during their sparring sessions; and although none of them would admit it, he was better at it than they were. If he'd been tasked with fighting another person—or even two—he would have given himself good odds.

But he'd never been taught how to battle a plant.

He firmed his grip on the hilt and took a last look at the raven. "My name's Morli, by the way. I'm from Udrodia. I love to bake. I really wish my life had turned out differently. Oh well. Here goes nothing." And, blade raised, he lunged at the bramble.

His sword was of excellent quality, forged by the finest craftsman in Udrodia. It sliced easily through even the thick branches, and for a brief time Morli almost believed he might succeed, if only he was fast enough.

But when he'd chopped a shallow tunnel into the briar, the vines began to rustle urgently. Several of them snaked across the tunnel entrance, shooting out new tendrils as he watched, cutting off his escape. He tried to slice them away, but thick vines twined around him. They pinned his arms to his body and squeezed him so tightly that he gasped for air. The sword fell from his hand and clanged on the hard ground. And then the vines were lifting him, raising him ten, fifteen, twenty feet into the air. He could see the distant smudge of the forest he'd passed through on the way here, but not Hendry or the horse. Maybe they'd already turned back. He tried to kick, but the vines had encircled his legs.

Thorns pierced him, dug all the way into his flesh, into his bones. He tried to scream, but now another vine was winding around his neck.

He managed one choked sob before he died.

"Do you mind if I eat your eyes?"

Morli was dead. He knew that immediately. Not just because he wasn't breathing and had no heartbeat, but because he had no... substance. He was still high in the bramble, the pain gone, but there was no *self* to him. He had less substance than a wisp of cloud. He wasn't scared anymore—what was left to be afraid of? The only thing keeping him from evaporating completely was a heavy portion of regret.

And the raven was talking to him, voice hoarse but completely understandable.

"My eyes?" Morli said. Well, not out loud because he had no lungs, no tongue, no mouth. But he thought it very clearly.

"You don't need them anymore," the raven said. "And they're tasty."

Morli appreciated that the raven had asked before digging in. "Help yourself."

The raven cawed happily and hopped closer. It was a substantial bird with shining black feathers, a heavy beak, and an intelligent gaze. "You shouldn't have tried to get through the bramble," it said.

"I know."

"Humans are remarkably stupid."

"I know that too."

The raven took a moment to preen one of its wings. "You're stubborn too. I mean, you're good and dead. I'll be eating your eyes in a minute. But you're still hanging around." It cocked its head. "Why?"

Morli would have shrugged if he had a body. "I'm not sure."

"I bet it's failed hopes. That often seems to be the case. You're disappointed you didn't get to marry the princess."

"Not especially. Is she even in there? Alive, I mean?"

The raven cawed something akin to a chuckle. "She's in there. Snoring away. That's part of the spell, you know. She sleeps until she's rescued. Otherwise maybe she'd find a way to get herself out. All your shouting was useless."

"Oh." The tiny bit of Morli that could still feel was relieved that at least she wasn't suffering. "You could have told me that when I was alive."

"You wouldn't have understood me when you were alive. So if it's not failing with the rescue that's got you haunting the place, what is it?"

Morli prodded at the chunk of regret to feel its shape. Oh. "Nobody loved me. And I never had a chance to love anyone else."

"Ah," said the raven. "That is rough. My mate and I were together for ten years. We fledged over thirty chicks together —he was an excellent father. Handsome too." She made a sorrowful sound. "And then some fool of a human shot him with an arrow. Why would anyone do that? My mate never harmed a human."

"I don't know. I'm sorry."

She turned a bright eye on him. "Have *you* ever killed a raven?"

"I've never killed anything." That was true. When he encountered spiders in the castle he ignored them or, if they seemed too intrusive, relocated them outside. He ignored the mice who lived in the pantry, even when they nibbled on his ingredients. Sometimes he even dropped them a crumb or two of bread.

The raven croaked. "I have. I've hunted to feed myself and my chicks. But I don't kill for sport."

"I'm sorry about your mate."

"Well, at least I had one. You should have seen his talons! So long! You know what they say about a male with long talons."

"Um...."

She cackled so hard she nearly fell off the branch, and then she had to ruffle her feathers back into place. "I like you. Most of the other corpses go on and on about themselves and lost glory. They complain when I eat them—as if they have any other use while they hang there and rot."

"You can eat me," said Morli, who figured he might as well serve some purpose.

"Thank you. Mind if I share? Some of my grown chicks are here."

"I guess there's plenty of me to go around." Morli, who had enjoyed sampling his own baked creations, was a little soft around the stomach.

"Excellent." She hunched her shoulders conspiratorially and lowered her voice to a hoarse whisper. "Your eyes are just for me, though. They're the best part."

"Bon appétit."

"You know... I haven't done this in a very long time. Not since before I met my mate. But I'm single now and my chicks are all fledged. Want to go on an adventure with me?"

"But... I'm dead." Weren't his adventures—minimal as they were—behind him?

She cackled again. "A minor obstacle. I can deal. Are you up for it?"

He figured he had nothing to lose. "Yeah. Sure."

"Outstanding!" She flapped her wings with excitement. "I'm in the mood for some excitement. But first I'm going to eat your eyes." With a contented little huff, she began to peck.

2

———

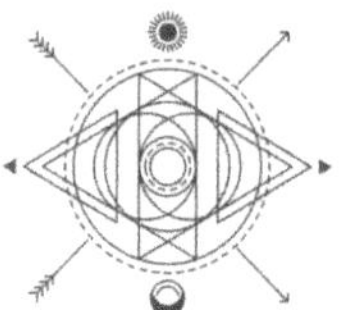

S*eptember 2020*
Modesto, California

Baxter Quirke shoved the Ouija board off his coffee table. It hadn't worked. He hadn't *expected* it to work, but some little part inside of him hoped it would, and that part was disappointed. No helpful messages from his great-aunt Opal, who'd always claimed that she was a witch and that Baxter had inherited her magical talents.

"Hah," he said, startling himself with the sound of his own voice. It had been a long time since he'd spoken aloud. If he *had* possessed any supernatural skills, such as premonition, he would have foreseen back in January that moving across the country was a bad idea. Sure, it had seemed like a good plan at the time. He'd recently broken up with Sven, a messy situation that had also cost him most of their mutual friends. His parents were... somewhere else, maybe New Hampshire. He'd had nothing in particular tying him to

Chicago, and when he'd gotten a job offer in California, he'd been filled with optimism.

Not a single little premonition to hint that a pandemic was on the way. No clue that just as he was getting settled into his small rented house on Drury Lane in Modesto, the state would go into lockdown, his job would go remote, and he'd be stuck all alone in a place where he knew nobody.

"You could have warned me, Aunt Opal!"

A loud buzzing startled him. For a split second he thought it might be Aunt Opal trying to communicate after all. But then he remembered that he had zucchini sourdough muffins baking, and the timer was going off. He hurried into the kitchen.

When Baxter had chosen the house, he hadn't paid much attention to the kitchen. Even though he could cook a few things like pasta and omelets, he tended to rely heavily on takeout. So his biggest concerns had been affordable rent and an easy commute to work. Well, now all he did was commute from his bedroom to the *other* bedroom, which contained his desk, so that wasn't an issue.

But like many other people confined to their homes, he'd dabbled in new hobbies. For one thing, he'd taken up baking, as a result of which he'd gained ten pounds and learned that his kitchen setup was far from ideal. Too cramped. Not enough work space. Too little storage. He managed anyway because he was bored and moving was out of the question, but he wished he had more counter space. Right now, for instance, setting out the cooling rack meant that he needed to temporarily put the plastic compost bucket on top of the fridge.

The muffins were fragrant, their lovely tan domes flecked with bits of green. The surface gave a bit under the pressure of his fingertip and then bounced back, just as it ought to. He was tempted to gobble one right away but knew it was best to let them cool for at least a few minutes. While they were not exactly low-cal, he'd convinced himself that they'd make healthy treats. Sourdough was supposed to be good for your gut bacteria, and this recipe also contained zucchini, which had vitamins and fiber.

Okay, maybe he could eat just one right now.

The muffin stuck to the paper liner, and he burned his fingers slightly trying to unpeel it, but the results were worth it. "Mmm. Tha' goo'," he announced with his mouth full. Maybe he wasn't any good with magic, but at least he could make tasty food.

Come to think of it, the recipe for these muffins had come from Great-aunt Opal. It was one of several dozen she'd written on index cards in her careful old-fashioned cursive, gifted to him when he first moved out on his own. Chicken-and-green-bean casserole, easy tuna pie, Swedish meatballs, meatloaf surprise (the surprise was a lava lake of melted cheese guaranteed to scorch your tongue), spice cookies, cornbread dressing. He'd prepared very few of the recipes, but simply reading them brought back fond memories of childhood sleepovers at Aunt Opal's house. Her sisters would join them for dinner—his great-aunt Ruby and his grandmother Pearl—the three of them cackling so happily they couldn't possibly be anything *but* witches. Then, after the other women left, Aunt Opal would let Baxter stay up way past his bedtime watching TV before tucking him into bed in a tiny room with a skylight that allowed him to fall asleep staring at the moon and stars.

"I miss you, Aunt Opal." That's why he'd tried to summon her with the Ouija board—he pined for her company and her advice, and dammit, he was just plain lonely.

Baxter realized that the muffin was gone and he was folding the paper liner into a messy, shapeless origami. He gazed at the liner's pattern—pink cupcakes surrounded by rainbow hearts—and then tossed it with a perfect arc into the compost bucket.

That was when he remembered another of the recipes Aunt Opal had given him. He'd laughed when he first saw it, dismissing it as one of her eccentricities. Now it took him a few minutes to find it in the recipe box, stuck to a card on how to make orange-glazed beets.

Happiness, the card title said. As if joy was just another thing you could whip up in the kitchen. But he certainly could use some happiness, and trying the recipe wasn't any more far-fetched than attempting to communicate with the dearly departed.

Baxter had most of the ingredients: cinnamon, sugar, black pepper, chili powder, lemon juice, almond extract. He didn't have any dragon's blood, however, and after a moment's consideration substituted fennel seed—because why not. As the recipe instructed, he mixed everything together in a small bowl, held it over his head, and spun around ten times counterclockwise while humming Steve Miller's "Abracadabra." The spell didn't actually specify the song, but he thought that one apt. Finally, he licked a finger, rolled it in the mixture, and slurped it clean.

Okay, it wasn't truly a recipe, more like a spell. Then again, Aunt Opal used to say that good cooking was a type of magic, so maybe the difference between recipes and spells was fuzzy.

In any case, it didn't work. Despite following the instructions—other than the dragon's blood substitution—he didn't feel any happier. In fact, he was somewhat *less* happy because the mixture tasted terrible. He sighed and dumped the contents of the bowl into the compost bucket, on top of the sourdough discard, zucchini ends, and cupcake liner. He would have made a trip out to the compost bin, except it was all the way across his backyard and he was wearing nothing but a pair of skimpy underwear. He'd bought them long ago to surprise Sven, but now in a fruitless demonstration of defiance and independence, he wore them around the house. Sometimes he even worked in them if he didn't have a Zoom meeting scheduled.

Baxter opened the back door halfway and peeked outside. A six-foot privacy fence surrounded his yard, which would have been great if the family next door didn't have a treehouse perched ten feet up a sturdy evergreen. It was a pretty nice treehouse, and he sort of envied the three kids who got to play in it. But it gave them a bird's-eye view of his yard, which meant clothing was not optional for him outside. Right now there was no sign of children, just a big black bird peering at him from the treehouse roof. But just in case the kids were hidden inside, peering through the window and waiting to be scarred for life by a man in his Andrew Christians, he left the bucket on his tiny back patio to deal with later.

Back inside the house, Baxter cleaned the kitchen and returned the Ouija set to its box. He ate another muffin. And then he stood in the middle of his living room, unsettled. He could have gone outside to garden—another pandemic hobby he'd acquired—except the temperature was currently over a hundred degrees and the air quality was poor because half the state was on fire. Working out was an option; he'd stuffed an exercise bike and some weights into the second bedroom, along with the desk and chair. Or he could Netflix without the chill. Read a book. Get ahead on the work assignment that wasn't due for another week. He could resume the knitting project he'd begun as yet another hobby in March and abandoned when the temperatures got too hot to want wool in his lap. Or scroll aimlessly on his phone.

None of these options appealed to him. He was so sick of his own company that he wanted to scream.

Somehow he found himself hunched at his desk, typing "magic supplies Modesto" into a search engine. He had no idea what he wanted to buy. A guide to communicating with one's dead relatives? A time-turner so he could go back to January and, knowing a pandemic was coming, plan accordingly? Maybe dragon's blood, so he could try Aunt Opal's happiness recipe again, this time with full accuracy.

In any case, he didn't expect to find a magic shop here. If he were in the Bay Area, maybe. Unusual retail outlets weren't too remarkable in San Francisco. But in Modesto?

And sure enough, his search produced nothing in town. But... wait. There was a single hit in nearby Turlock. Marden's Magic Emporium. Huh.

Baxter clicked on the link, but all he got was an address and store hours. The website didn't say anything about what the shop carried or whether it was even operating now. He'd lost track of which businesses were and weren't allowed to have customers during the current stage of the pandemic. Did a magic emporium qualify as an essential business?

"This is really stupid, Baxter Quirke," he muttered as he keyed the shop's address into his phone. After putting on jeans and a plain red T-shirt that used to be baggy but now wasn't, he slipped into his sneakers. From a hook near the back door, he grabbed a face mask—this one said VOTE!— and walked toward the garage.

BAXTER'S PHONE directed him off the freeway and into Turlock, past a long chain of strip malls. Safeway, Target, Home Depot, Old Navy, an In-N-Out that might have tempted him if he hadn't already pigged out on sourdough zucchini muffins. "Turn right," the app ordered, and he did, into a parking lot shared by a pet supply store, Forever 21, and Dick's Sporting Goods. Hardly the location where he'd expect to find anything magical, but this was the correct address according to the website.

He parked, hooked the mask over his ears, and got out of the car. This was likely a fool's errand, but at least it had gotten him out of the house, which had probably been his unconscious goal to begin with. But the air felt like a convection oven and smelled of smoke even through the mask. He should give it up and go back home.

Just as he turned around and reached for the door handle, a large black bird swooped close to his head, startling him. When he twisted his neck to see where the bird went— Whoa. What was *that*?

Between the wide glass windows of a shoe outlet and a home goods store was a narrow space covered in what looked like carved wood panels. There was a wooden door, arched at the top and criss-crossed with heavy beams. And the entire door was *glowing*—purply-pink, like the glow sticks used at parties and on Halloween.

"Okay then," he whispered. There were several other cars in the big lot, but not a single other human was in sight. Baxter didn't know if that was a good thing or a bad one.

His heart beating rapidly, he made his way to the glowing door. There was no sign, no posted hours. But when he gave a light tug on the thick iron handle, the door swung open so easily that he almost lost his balance. He took a deep breath and stepped inside.

3

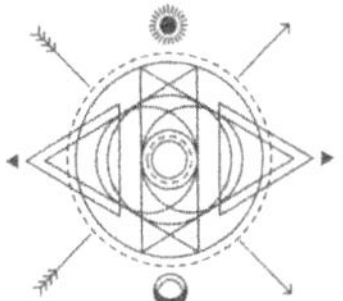

The inside of Marden's Magic Emporium was much larger than the outside. There was no way this vast space fit between the shoe store and the place that sold Live Laugh Love throw pillows. Yet here he was, and for several moments Baxter simply stood and gaped, wondering if he'd somehow accidentally included a hallucinogen in his sourdough zucchini muffins.

The place had a strong but pleasant smell: lemony, with hints of wax and herbs. In fact, it smelled a lot like Aunt Opal's house. But unlike her house, it was dusty, and trails of purple incense smoke crept under the ceiling, making Baxter sneeze. One corner held bubbling cauldrons—honest-to-god cauldrons, like props from Macbeth—while candles that surely violated the fire code flickered on shelves. Other shelves held old books and an array of knick-knacks that made Baxter uneasy if he looked too closely. Was that a shrunken head?

Blinking rapidly didn't make the store appear any more rational. He had just decided to back away, hightail it to his car, and return to his muffins and garden and unfinished knitting, when a man appeared in the doorway behind the counter. His flowing robes and Gandalf beard would have looked ridiculous anywhere else, but they perfectly fit the surrounding décor. He stared at Baxter with no particular expression on his wrinkled face.

"Uh, hi," Baxter said. He always felt uncomfortable when he browsed a store without buying something, as if the clerk might feel personally offended. And this was even worse because the man seemed to be sizing him up. Baxter tried to think of an excuse for a hasty exit. Should he point out that the guy wasn't wearing a mask, a probable violation of Governor Newsom's orders? What was the proper social distancing protocol in a store that, according to a tastefully lettered scroll hanging on one wall, was offering a special discount on wyvern scales?

"Um," Baxter said.

The wizard—he had to be a wizard, right?—turned his head and nodded at a woman who stood behind the counter. She looked like a goth poster girl: jet black hair that hung to her waist, a dark lace-up bodice over a black blouse, and a long black skirt. She didn't seem to be wearing any makeup and had the palest complexion Baxter had ever seen. She nodded back at the wizard, who disappeared through the doorway, and then she came out from behind the counter and walked toward Baxter.

"Welcome to Marden's Magic Emporium." She had a thick accent Baxter couldn't place, and possibly also a slight lisp. "I'm Ilona. Come, let me help you."

"I, uh, was just browsing."

When she laughed, her fangs showed. "Come with me."

Maybe they were fake fangs. Probably. And her crimson eyes were undoubtedly contact lenses. He followed her along a path laid out with glittery arrows, around a humungous stone mermaid and toward the long counter. He didn't see any other customers, which was disconcerting, but a couple of other employees watched him. Like Ilona and the wizard, they were apparently into cosplay too. One was a curvy woman with a white braid and pointy ears, while the other, an extremely tall and handsome man, had horns. They remained at their end of the counter, though, the tall guy bending down so his coworker could whisper something in his ear.

Ilona grinned at Baxter from behind the counter. "I like your mask. Is that your name on it—Votay?"

He goggled for a moment. "No. It's *vote*. As in an election."

"Ooh, I've heard about those! What are you voting for?"

Was she serious? "We're trying to preserve our democracy from a rising wave of fascism."

"Sounds fun! Very quaint. All right, let's get you set."

"I don't need anything. I'm here by accident." Should he take the lie further and claim he'd been looking for a potpourri bowl or running shoes?

"Oh, darling, if you're here, you need something. Let's find out what."

She pulled out a big burlap sack and set it on the stone countertop. The bag looked old and well-used. Then she stuck her hand inside, rummaged a bit, and came out with a slip of paper between her long, pale fingers. She squinted at it. "Huh."

"What does that mean?"

"Your item is in the revivarium room. I don't often go in there. Aisle twelve, bin...." She peered at the paper again. "Bin 27G."

"What item?"

"The one you need, of course. Follow me!"

He didn't want to. But he couldn't think of any way to extricate himself from this situation without feeling horribly awkward, so he followed as she opened a huge door and walked down a long corridor lined with swords. All that shining, sharp steel made Baxter uneasy, so he was considerably relieved when they passed through a small crooked doorway and into a narrow stone-walled hallway, dimly lit by cobwebby lanterns and interrupted at intervals by more doors. Maybe it was just a trick of the darkness, but the hall seemed to extend for miles.

"I don't understand how all of this is inside a strip mall," Baxter said. He almost tripped over an enormous, frayed rope that was partially uncoiled. "And how you guys aren't getting sued for a hundred safety violations."

Ilona didn't answer. But after a few yards more, she stopped in front of a door with *Revivarium* painted in gold letters.

"What does that mean?" Baxter asked.

"Just what it sounds like. A place where formerly living things find new uses. Or parts of formerly living things."

He did not like the sound of that. It was worse than the swords. Yet somehow he followed her into a vast room that reminded him of Costco: concrete floors, a tall ceiling with fluorescent lights, sturdy towering metal shelves. Each row had a number at the end, and the shelves themselves held big galvanized metal bins, each with a lid and a number-letter combination stenciled on its front. Baxter was thankful he couldn't see what was inside.

In aisle twelve, Ilona hummed as she counted her way to 27. Bin G was on the shelf nearest the ground. "Let's see," she trilled, bending to remove the lid. She was the cheeriest goth vampire cosplayer Baxter had ever met. And he'd met quite a few, thanks to sci-fi cons.

Ilona reached deep into the bin and, hesitating just enough to make Baxter nervous, pulled out... a manila envelope.

"That's anticlimactic." Baxter said. He had been expecting bones. Or skin. Ooh, maybe a book bound in human skin! Or a potion made from newt eyeballs and lizard legs. But he took the envelope from her outstretched hand and opened the flap to look.

"Feathers?" He started to reach inside.

"Don't touch them!"

Baxter startled so violently that he bounced back against the shelf, bruising his shoulder. At least he didn't drop the envelope. "What? What's wrong?"

"What color are they?"

"Black."

Ilona nodded. "Raven."

"What does that mean?"

"They have a lot of power. But they're..."—she scrunched up her mouth and waggled a hand—"tricky. How many do you have?"

He peered into the envelope. "Three?"

"Each of those has the potential for strong magic. But you can use them only once, so don't touch them until you need them."

"Need them for what? How am I supposed to use them?"

Ilona shrugged. "That's the tricky part. You never know with raven feathers. Best to go with what your gut tells you."

In Baxter's experience, his gut was really good at telling him it wanted feeding and not so great at anything else. After all, if his gut were so smart, he wouldn't be stranded in Modesto all by his lonesome. And he wouldn't have made this excursion to the magic emporium.

Without another word, Ilona took him back to the big

room where he'd entered. The tall man and elf-eared woman still stood there. He had the impression that the minute he was gone, they'd interrogate Ilona about him and his envelope. For her part, Ilona consulted a scroll that had been stored behind the counter. "Let's see... auk, dodo, firebird, griffin, harpy, phoenix, quetzalcoatl... ah, there we go, raven." She looked up at Baxter. "That's nineteen ninety-five. If you don't have the cash we can trade for something."

"None of those things exist except the raven. Um, and maybe the auk."

She scoffed. "Is that so? Then I guess vampires don't exist either. Or elves or incubi." She gestured at the two other employees. "There's a lot more going on in the worlds than you think, foolish mortal. Do you need a bag?"

"Uh... no. Thanks." And since she seemed to be waiting, he dug in his wallet and fished out a twenty-dollar bill, which he set on the counter.

She tucked it into a cash box. "Darn, we're out of nickels. Will you take a groat instead?" She held up a small silver coin.

"You can keep the change."

"Bye, Baxter. Good luck!"

Smiling dazedly and clutching the manila envelope, he emerged into sweltering heat and an ash-gray sky. He was halfway back to Modesto when it occurred to him that he'd never told Ilona his name.

4

He regretted skipping In-N-Out. It hadn't been all that long since he'd eaten the muffins, but it *felt* like forever, thanks to his weird adventure in Turlock. He decided he deserved a treat, especially since he rarely ate restaurant food anymore, and so he detoured to a Middle Eastern place. He got chicken shawarma, falafel, and baklava to go, feeling only a brief pang of nostalgia for the good old days when he used to eat in restaurants with friends.

Back home, he enjoyed his little feast in the living room in front of the TV, where he streamed the new season of *Lucifer*. He cared less about the plot than about watching Tom Ellis. And listening to his accent. Although that was diverting for a while, images on a screen—even very handsome images—could do only so much.

The truth was, Baxter was so lonely he wanted to cry.

He'd never been all that great at meeting people. He felt too awkward around others, too afraid he'd say or do something stupid. As a kid, he'd hung back in crowds. He was the quiet kid in the back of the classroom, the one who got good grades and nobody noticed. He'd made two close friends in college, but one had freaked minor hysterics and backed away when Baxter came out. Baxter had stayed friends with the other for longer, but then they'd had a nasty fight after the 2016 election and had never reconciled.

His love life had been equally unpromising—quick hookups and nothing else—until he met Sven. At the gym. Oh God, he'd met a guy named Sven at the gym and actually expected things to turn out well, as if Sven would be the love of his life. And the thing was, Sven was a good guy, and he was hot as hell, and the two of them were fantastic in bed together. The problem was with all the time when they weren't in bed; they had little in common. Sven called him a nerd when Baxter wanted to watch Dr. Who or a Marvel movie. Sven didn't even know the difference between *Star Wars* and *Star Trek*, and he didn't care. He thought they were both for children. They didn't even have the same interests in food. Nor the same vision for the future. When Baxter pushed for something more substantial between them, Sven started becoming more distant, and that eventually led to the end.

"Someday this pandemic will be over," Baxter informed Tom Ellis. "I'll have the chance to meet people in person instead of on Zoom. I will acquire a small but close friendship circle, and I will find true love."

Tom Ellis scoffed, and Baxter couldn't blame him.

Maybe Baxter should find an additional pandemic hobby. He had more zucchini, tomatoes, and peppers than he knew what to do with; baking was going well; and he had a nice yarn stash waiting for him once the temperatures dropped. The only pastime he'd failed at had been magic, and in retrospect, maybe attempting to communicate with his favorite but dead relative wasn't such a great idea anyway. Aunt Opal deserved to rest in peace—or have a really great time in the afterlife—without worrying about Baxter and his stupid problems.

Okay, then. What to choose for his new hobby? He could take an online course on postmodern philosophy or chicken behavior, neither of which he knew anything about. He could learn to play the ukulele. He could set up a wood-working shop in the garage and make cuckoo clocks and refinish furniture. Was beekeeping legal inside the city limits? Stargazing might be fun, except he wasn't going to see any stars until the wildfire smoke cleared. Jigsaw puzzles. Beermaking. Yoga?

"Ugh," Baxter said to Tom Ellis and flopped back on the couch to stare at the ceiling. He knew he was lucky; he had a good job, a nice place to live, and his health. Self-pity was not a good hobby.

When he sat up again, the manila envelope with the feathers caught his eye. He'd set it on an end table when he came home and promptly forgot about it, but now he was almost surprised to discover it really existed and that he hadn't just dreamed that really weird experience. There must have been something he'd missed; maybe Marden's was a theme experience. Kind of like an escape room, only instead of solving clues you pretended you'd stepped into a Terry Pratchett novel. And Baxter had taken the bait, docilely shelling out twenty bucks for three feathers.

Feeling slightly swindled, he tapped at his phone in search of more information about Marden's Magic Emporium. He found... nothing. The website he'd visited earlier in the day didn't exist, according to his browser. Search engines found nothing. And when he brought up a map of the strip mall in Turlock, it showed the shoe store directly next to the home goods place, with nothing in between.

Jesus, maybe the solitude was making Baxter halluci-
nate. Except if none of that had really happened, where had
the feathers come from?

Wanting to make sure he hadn't simply procured the
envelope from his stash of office supplies while in some sort
of fugue state, Baxter picked it up and opened it. He stuck in
his hand and pulled out... a feather. It was roughly eight
inches long, with shiny black barbs and a white shaft. He
held it by the quill and trailed the soft tip over his cheeks,
shivering a little at the tickling sensation. The feather had
no smell and no discernible weight, but it was, as far as he
could tell, entirely real.

"Weird mysteries are also not a pandemic hobby I want
to take up," he said to the feather. Because if you can talk to
the broadcast image of an actor playing the devil, you can
just as easily talk to a bird part. "All I want is... happiness. Is
that so much to ask?"

For one terrifying moment, the feather glowed like lava.
Then it crumbled to ash and was gone.

That was just too much. Although it was early, he
decided to call it a night. Surely in the morning everything
would be back to boring old normal. He might even get
some work done, even though it would be Sunday.

After he gathered the takeout food wrappers and
deposited them into the kitchen trash, he stood and considered whether to have another muffin—a nightcap of sorts
—when a crash and yell came from just outside the back
door.

A burglar! Baxter grabbed the nearest weapon-like
thing, which turned out to be his rolling pin, raised it high,
and waited for someone to come bursting through the
locked door. Nobody did, which he supposed was a good
thing. He should probably fetch his phone and call the

police. Before he could move, however, another sound came from outside: a long, low moan.

Had the burglar hurt himself? Good. Then maybe he'd go away.

Baxter slowly lowered the rolling pin but otherwise remained frozen, his ears perked for any subsequent outdoor sounds. Nothing. He suddenly pictured a would-be burglar lying on the concrete patio, bleeding out after having tripped and bashed his head. That was awful, and not just because Baxter didn't want a corpse in his backyard. Nobody deserved to die like that, even if they were a burglar.

After a few additional seconds of painful indecision, and still clutching the rolling pin, Baxter walked to the door. He turned on the porch light, unfastened the lock, and opened the door, his heart beating so loudly that he could hardly hear anything else. Most of the yard was dark and the air reeked of smoke, but the lightbulb cast a circle of bright illumination just outside the door.

A man lay on his back on the patio, unmoving.

The first thing Baxter noticed was that the man's left foot was stuck in the compost bucket, as if it were some absurd type of shoe. The second notable thing was that the man's long, wavy hair was dark green, which wouldn't have been especially remarkable except the hair on the man's groin was *also* dark green. Baxter had never heard of anyone dyeing their pubic hair. And that led to the third thing he noticed—which really should have been the first—which was that, apart from the compost bucket, the man was stark naked.

That was a really odd way to commit burglary.

Raising the rolling pin again, Baxter took a cautious step out the door, and then another. He didn't see any sign of blood, which he supposed was a good thing. But of course not all injuries bled, and not all bleeding was obvious. Maybe the guy had a concussion. Or an internal bleed. Either of those would technically be Baxter's fault for leaving the bucket on an unlit patio.

"Um, hello?"

Baxter breathed more easily when the man's eyes fluttered open. They were remarkable eyes, the same green as the hair. Contacts? Was this guy a cosplayer too? "Did you follow me home from Marden's?" Baxter demanded, brandishing the rolling pin. "Is this more of the con?"

The man whimpered and rolled into a protective ball.

Another light shot out from the darkness, this one wavering. A flashlight coming from the neighbors' treehouse. Were the kids up there now, watching Baxter loom over some naked guy? Shit. Baxter thought about marching back inside, locking the door, and calling the cops. But that would leave the mystery man outside in the smoky air, possibly hurt, with no clothing, and with the neighbor kids looking on. Moreover, the guy didn't seem dangerous. Baxter was over six feet tall, had always been fairly muscular, and had recently gained additional baking weight. He was quite a bit larger than the other man, who very clearly wasn't armed.

"Can you walk?" Baxter tried to sound gentle instead of scared and confused.

After a long pause, the man uncurled, blinked up at him, and whispered, "Wh-where am I?" He looked at his own arms and down at his body before gazing again at Baxter. "I'm not dead."

"No, but let's get you inside and make sure you're not hurt."

Very slowly, eyes wide and dazed, the man pulled the bucket off and got to his feet. He was shivering violently despite the still-warm night. Drugs maybe—which would explain quite a bit, in fact. He didn't look like an addict, though. But then, what did Baxter know?

Somewhat theatrically, Baxter gestured at the door. "Come on in."

The man shuffled forward. He moved awkwardly, as if he weren't used to his body, and cringed slightly as he passed Baxter and his rolling pin. As the guy was stepping inside, Baxter got a good look at the tattoo on one rather nice butt cheek: a pink cupcake surrounded by rainbow hearts.

5

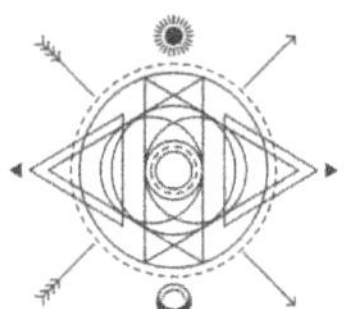

The man's name was Morli; they'd gotten that far, although he couldn't seem to produce a last name and simply shook his head when Baxter asked. But the fact that he remembered a name at all meant he didn't have amnesia. Or so Baxter hoped. He had an accent that Baxter couldn't place. Possibly something British, but maybe not.

And he certainly didn't seem scary as he huddled on Baxter's couch, wrapped in the throw blanket Baxter had knitted on size 35 needles before the weather turned too hot for yarn. He did look deeply confused, however, his mouth hanging open and his eyes blinking as he gazed around the room.

Morli was also very handsome, although Baxter shouldn't have been noticing. But his green hair and eyes were set off nicely by his light tan skin, and he had a sweet mouth, the type you really wanted to see curled in a smile.

"Thank you," Morli said when Baxter handed him a glass of water. He took several swallows. "This isn't the inside of the tower, is it?"

"What tower?"

"The one with the princess."

Oookay. "I doubt very much that there are any princesses in Modesto."

"Modesto." Morli tasted the name on his tongue. "Is that the name of this kingdom?"

Baxter decided he should be the one asking questions. "What were you doing in my yard? And where are your clothes?"

"I... I was in the bramble."

"I don't know what you're talking about."

"The vines and the... the thorns. And the raven who ate my eyes. She was nice." Morli looked around. "Where did she go?"

Drugs or mental illness, Baxter decided. He should probably call the cops. But then Morli would end up in jail or some other facility, not great places to be with Covid lurking about. Plus, he seemed so frightened and vulnerable. What if the police were unkind? Everyone was so on edge lately.

"Would you like to spend the night here? We can get you squared away in the morning."

It was a foolish offer, maybe one of the dumbest things Baxter had ever done. But he didn't feel threatened by this poor guy. Maybe after a night's sleep Morli would be more in his right mind, and Baxter could figure out where he belonged. Morli's people might be looking for him.

"I... I can stay here?"

"If you want."

Morli gave him a tentative smile. "Thank you. I don't understand what's happening."

That makes two of us, dude.

"Are you hungry?" Baxter asked.

Morli seemed to consider for a moment. "No. But...." His cheeks colored. "Can you show me where the garderobe is?"

Now, it so happened that when Baxter was ten or eleven, he'd gone through a Medieval phase in which he read about knights and nobility and castles. So he knew what a garderobe was, although he'd never expected to hear the term in twenty-first-century California. "You mean the bathroom?"

"I... I don't think I want to bathe just now, thank you. I, um... I need to urinate."

They could figure out the weird terminology in the morning. "Follow me," Baxter said.

But when they reached what Baxter thought of as the guest bathroom—despite his usual lack of guests—Morli looked bewildered. Baxter had to explain how to use the toilet. The flush made Morli startle, then stare at the swirling water, but then he became fascinated by the sink. "Warm water! Is it bespelled?" He turned the faucet on and off.

"No. There's a water heater in the garage." Baxter answered almost absently. At first he'd been unwillingly charmed by Morli's bizarre wonder over everyday things, and now he was distracted because Morli... smelled. Not bad. Not at all the way you'd expect a naked junkie burglar to smell, but actually very pleasant. Morli smelled like fresh-baked bread.

Baxter realized he was leaning in and sniffling, so he hurriedly took a step back. Morli didn't even notice, however, because he'd caught his reflection in the mirror. He slowly stroked his cheek. "That's not me," he whispered. He caught Baxter's gaze. "Is... is the glass enchanted?"

"It's just a regular mirror."

Morli made a small, wounded noise before whirling to

face him. "Why is my hair that color?" He looked on the verge of tears.

"I don't know."

"But.... What...." Morli bowed his head, which turned out to be a mistake because he caught sight of his own groin. He hadn't focused on it while peeing because he'd been too busy admiring the toilet, but now he saw that the carpet matched the drapes, so to speak. He gave a little wail and collapsed to the floor.

Heart twisting, Baxter crouched in front of him. "Hey, it's no big deal. You look good in green."

Morli wasn't comforted. "I'm not real. I don't know what.... Do you know what I am?"

"A guy who's had a rough night and needs some sleep. C'mon. Everything will look brighter in the morning." Deep in his heart, Baxter suspected several parts of that were inaccurate. But he knew from his own experiences that when disaster struck, being slapped in the face with the Fish of Cold Hard Truth wasn't pleasant. God knew he'd wished someone had been around to hand him empty platitudes when his life fell apart.

After a moment, Morli gave a slow nod. "Thank you." He climbed awkwardly to his feet and shambled back to the living room, then watched dull-eyed while Baxter made up the couch with sheets, a pillow, and a light blanket. The couch didn't pull out into a bed, but it wasn't too bad to sleep on for a single night.

"Want to borrow some clothes?"

The reply was almost too quiet to hear. "Yes, please."

Baxter gave him his softest old T-shirt. It was a favorite, but due to Baxter's carb consumption, it would likely be a little too snug now. Morli stared at the image on the front— the house from *Up* floating away with balloons—but apparently decided it was just another unfathomable mystery. He put on the shirt and the gray sweats Baxter gave him, and then he lay down on the couch with a long sigh.

"If you need me, I'll be in my bedroom." Baxter pointed, even though the location was fairly obvious. It wasn't a big house. And due to the suspicion he was still trying to ignore, he added, "Do you know how to turn off the lights?"

Morli shook his head.

So Baxter did it for him and then spent a moment standing awkwardly in the darkness, clutching his phone. "Good night."

"You're being very kind to me. Thank you."

"I'm glad I can help." Which was the truth.

It took Baxter a long time to fall asleep, and not because he was afraid Morli was going to murder him. He couldn't possibly explain why, but he trusted Morli. Hell, there wasn't any rational explanation for most of the things that had happened that day. But it was kind of nice to have some company, even if the company was... very strange.

Baxter fell asleep thinking about Morli's tattoo.

6

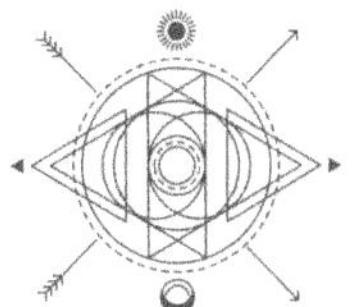

Even if things didn't look any brighter in the morning, they felt a lot clearer. At some point while Baxter slept, his subconscious had apparently decided that his best option was to accept the impossible. He marched into the living room with a sense of purpose.

But when he arrived, he paused. Morli still slept, the blanket tucked up to his chin, his green hair arrayed over the pillow. He looked innocent and very handsome, and the entire living room smelled like fresh bread. When his eyes fluttered open and he saw Baxter, he gave a sunny smile—which quickly faded. His astonishing eyes filled with distress. "Wh-where...?"

"It's okay. You're in my house in Modesto, remember? And I'm Baxter."

That seemed to steady Morli a bit. He sat up and swung his feet to the floor. "I'll go now. Thank you for your hospitality. May I keep the clothing? I don't...." He trailed off hopelessly.

Baxter made his voice soft. "Do you have somewhere to go?"

"No."

"Then stay here for the time being."

"I don't want to inconvenience you."

"You're not. I'm happy to have you." Baxter waved toward the kitchen. "How about some breakfast?"

Morli managed the bathroom by himself this time. He gaped at the kitchen, which he'd been too dazed to notice the previous night, but he didn't ask about anything. Instead he sat at the little table across from Baxter and eyed what was in front of him. "I'm sorry. I don't mean to be rude, but I'm unfamiliar with these things."

That didn't surprise Baxter. "Zucchini muffin and coffee."

Although Morli nodded politely, those words obviously meant nothing to him. He took a careful sip of coffee and hastily set the mug back down. "I...."

"Maybe you should try it with milk and sugar."

But even though Baxter added a *lot* of milk and sugar—so much that the liquid was barely tan—Morli was politely horrified. Grinning to himself, Baxter poured him a glass of iced tea instead. Morli was delighted. "How have you found ice when it's warm outside? More magic?"

"Something like that," said Baxter, who didn't really know how freezers worked. For all he knew, enchantments *were* involved.

Morli swirled the glass to make the cubes clink and then took several large swallows. "Delicious!" But it was the muffin that truly engaged him. He watched closely as Baxter peeled away the cupcake liner, then mimicked him. "It's a cake?" Morli poked at it gently.

"Pretty much. It's a muffin. Which is mostly like a cake

but maybe a little less sweet? And it has some vegetable inside so we can pretend it's healthy." Muffins were also less fluffy than cupcakes, but that was probably more detail than Morli needed.

Morli didn't eat it right away, setting it on his palm and examining it closely, the way a jeweler might look at a new gem. Only Baxter seemed to notice that the flecks of zucchini were the precise color of his hair and eyes. Morli poked the muffin a few more times and sniffed it before finally breaking off a crumb and placing it on his tongue. "Oh! That's very good." He took a bigger bite this time but savored it slowly. "Your baker is very talented. I wonder if they could show me how to make these."

Baxter grinned. "I made them."

That seemed to delight Morli. "Really? You're a baker?"

"Not professionally. It's something I do for fun."

"Me too!" Morli's face fell. "Well, I used to."

"Would you like to try some of my bread? It's two days old, but it'll be good if I toast it."

As they ate, they had a conversation about various baking ingredients and techniques. It was clear that Morli knew a lot more about the subject than Baxter, and also that Morli didn't exactly buy his flour at the nearest Safeway. But at least he seemed intrigued by the things Baxter told him instead of lost and terrified. And it was a nice temporary distraction from more pressing matters.

Eventually, however, the conversation had to turn away from baking. Baxter poured more coffee for himself and tea for Morli, and they looked at each other over the table. "Can you tell me where you're from, Morli? And what happened to you. I, uh, think magic is involved."

That last bit actually seemed to reassure Morli. "Yes, it definitely is." Then he launched into his tale.

Baxter interrupted often with questions—"Wait! You're a *prince*? Like honest-to-God royalty?"—so the story took a long time. And it was a very sad story, Baxter thought, although he admired Morli's courage and dignity. Had Baxter been in his position, he would have headed for the hills and lived as a peasant instead of trying to get into the tower, knowing he'd fail and die. And Morli had died, which broke Baxter's heart despite the fact that Morli was sitting right here and chatting with him.

"Raven, huh?"

"Yes," Morli said. "I don't mind that she ate my eyes. She was polite about it."

The odd thing wasn't that Morli was royalty from a seemingly alternate universe, or that he'd had a starring role in a fairy tale, or even that he'd somehow ended up in Modesto. The odd thing was that Baxter didn't doubt a word of the completely unbelievable tale. Given what the rest of this year had been like, maybe he shouldn't be surprised.

"That's all I know," Morli said as he finished off his third muffin. "I don't understand what happened to me."

"I don't either. But I have some theories."

Morli's eyes shone. "Yes?"

"Have you noticed the design on the cupcake liner?" Baxter held up one of the leftover muffins.

"Yes...." But Morli seemed uncertain.

"Come with me." Together they marched to Baxter's bedroom, where a full-length mirror hung behind the door. "Um, pull down your waistband a little and look at your butt." Baxter felt himself blushing.

"What?"

"Easier to show than explain."

Confused and maybe a little skeptical, Morli obeyed. He gasped when he saw the tattoo. "That's— How— What...."

"The same as the cupcake liner, right?"

"Why?" It came out nearer a wail than a question.

It was better to do this with Morli sitting down, so Baxter gently guided him to the edge of the mattress and then remained standing while Morli perched.

"So is magic a pretty common thing where you come from?"

"Common? Only those with special skills can do enchantments. Just as only some people can bake well."

"Yeah, all right, but there are lots of bakers. How many, um, magic-users are there? I mean, do you encounter them often?"

Morli nodded thoughtfully. "Yes, I suppose so. My parents have three royal sorcerers."

Three. Was that a lot? And were there special standards for being a royal sorcerer instead of an ordinary everyday one? Maybe there were different grades of sorcerership. *Focus, Baxter.* "The thing is, magic isn't common here. Most people don't believe in it."

That made Morli laugh. "Not believe in it? That's ridiculous. It's like not believing in the moons."

Moons, plural? Okay, not relevant at the moment. "But it's rare here. Most people never see it at all."

"Do *you* believe in it?"

"Yeah. My great-aunt Opal was a witch." He didn't add that, even so, his belief had been shaky until this morning. "She probably wasn't up to royal sorcerer levels, but she and her coven would do little spells now and then. You know, useful things, like finding lost items or helping someone's insomnia."

"She would not entrap a princess or murder people with a bramble?" Morli seemed completely serious.

"Absolutely not. Aunt Opal was a nice person. Swore like

a sailor—God, my parents hated that—but she was the type of person who'd go to the animal shelter and adopt the pets nobody wanted. The ancient, incontinent, blind chihuahuas and the cats that scratched you if you tried to pet them. She gave money to children's charities and marched for civil rights." And, Baxter didn't add, she gave him a safe and loving environment when things became too much at home.

But Morli was chewing his lip, and Baxter realized he'd allowed the conversation to veer off course. "Anyway, she left me a spell and I tried it for the first time yesterday. And after that... things got weird. I ended up at this very strange magic shop that doesn't officially exist, where I bought three feathers for twenty bucks. Three *raven* feathers."

"Oh." Morli thought about that for a moment. "Why did you buy them?"

"I have no idea. The sales clerk said I needed them. Um, she might be a vampire." He shook his head to clear it. "Anyway, I was touching one of those feathers last night when you... appeared. And the feather sort of went *fzzz*." He moved his hands in a completely inaccurate and unhelpful demonstration.

Morli didn't seem in the mood to judge Baxter's acting skills, however. He was staring at his own hands, turning them this way and that, and then he pulled a strand of hair forward so he could examine it as well. "The raven brought me here," he said, brow furrowed. "I think I understand that. But where is here? And what happened to... my body?" He shuddered. "It was dead. *I* was dead. But...."

"I think that's the issue. Your... youness wasn't connected to your body anymore. And probably the raven didn't want to stick you back in, um, well, a corpse."

"With no eyes," Morli said sadly. "And lots of holes from the bramble. That would have been awful."

Baxter pushed away a terrible vision of Morli dying in agony, hanging from the vines and pierced by countless thorns. "Do you hurt now?"

"No, not at all. I feel good." He rolled his shoulders experimentally. "Very good, in fact. But where did this body come from? I didn't displace anyone, did I?" He looked horrified.

"No, no. I think...." He took a deep breath. "You know those muffins we were eating?"

"Yes."

Jeez. How to put this delicately and without sounding like a complete lunatic? "When I made the muffins, I had some sourdough discard. The excess starter I had to get rid of after feeding it. Right?"

Morli nodded. "Of course." They'd already established that he was familiar with live starters in baking and, in fact, had never heard of the dried yeast Baxter often used instead.

"I put the discard into a little plastic bucket that I use to collect food scraps and things before taking them out to the compost bin. The end pieces of the zucchini were in there too. And also a torn-up cupcake liner—with a design that matches your tattoo. I set the bucket on the back porch yesterday afternoon and forgot about it."

Based on Morli's expression, he didn't want to hear the rest. And Baxter wasn't sure he wanted to say it. He was awkward with people under normal circumstances, and there had been nothing normal about the past twenty-four hours. But even though he'd been seriously weirded out and presented with a surprise houseguest, poor Morli's journey had been—and still was—unimaginable. At the very least, Morli deserved to know his own story.

"I think," Baxter said carefully, "somehow the raven—or

the feathers, or Aunt Opal's spell, or maybe all of the above —transported you here and, um, made you animate the contents of my compost bucket."

Morli simply blinked at him for a few moments. "Animate?"

"Starter is alive, isn't it? Full of... I don't know. Fungus or bacteria or something. And it grows. A few weeks ago I had a batch of starter overflow the container overnight. Big mess on the counter in the morning. So maybe the raven or the magic, or whatever, needed to stick you into something living but didn't want to squish you into another person's body. So they built you a new body out of some handy materials."

"A... new... body...." Morli said it very slowly.

"Your skin is the same shade as a bread crust, and your hair and eyes, they're zucchini green. Then there's your tattoo. And you smell nice, like baking bread." Oops. He hadn't intended to say that. His cheeks flamed and he avoided eye contact.

Morli lifted his arm and sniffed it. Then he sniffed again. "I do." And then he surprised Baxter by giving a small smile. "It's my favorite scent."

Baxter nodded and then stood there, unsure what else to say. Morli looked so lost and confused, and who could blame him. His entire existence had been turned upside down and inside out. Now he was all alone in an alien world, with not even a set of clothing to call his own. It occurred to Baxter, however, that he could help a little. "Hey. You can stay here, okay? As long as you want."

"Why would you offer that to me?"

Huh. Why would he? Unlike Aunt Opal, Baxter didn't take in strays. He didn't give shelter to lost souls. But now he had the chance to do just that, which would be an excellent way to honor Aunt Opal's memory. And that was appropriate, especially considering she probably had a part in putting Morli into Baxter's hands. "Some company would be nice," Baxter said with honesty. "I've been lonely."

"I have no money. No skills except baking. I can't…. Even my own parents had no use for me except to throw me at the bramble."

"You're my guest—you don't need to pay your way. But if you want, you could bake us some bread."

That tiny smile reappeared. God, Morli was beautiful. Baxter wished he wouldn't keep noticing that.

"May I have some time?" Morli asked hesitantly. "It's so much to consider. I hardly know what to think."

"In my opinion, you're showing incredible calm. And of course you can have some time. Look, stay here in the bedroom if you want, or hang out in the living room or whatever. I'm going to do some cycling, and afterward I'll probably catch up on some work in there." He pointed at the spare bedroom across the hall. "Let me know if you need anything."

"Thank you, Baxter. I'm very lucky I ended up at your home."

Those words warmed Baxter for hours.

7

Baxter had just demonstrated how the oven control panel worked, and now Morli touched it with great reverence. "That is amazing! You say you don't have much magic, but this seems like magic to me."

"It's not. It's technology. I don't know enough to explain it, but it's, you know, science. With rules."

"Magic has rules too."

True enough. Maybe magic was simply a very specialized sort of science, and most people denied its existence because they didn't understand it. "Well, one way or the other, it's handy."

"Will you show me how you make bread? Please?"

Baxter couldn't refuse, not when Morli's expression was so bright and eager. And if it helped Morli to avoid dwelling on his predicament for a little bit, even better. Not that he *was* dwelling, at least as far as Baxter could tell. He'd spent a couple of hours resting in Baxter's bedroom, but by the time Baxter emerged from his spare room, Morli was prowling the house, visually examining everything with great interest. Had Baxter been in his position, he would have curled into a ball and sobbed, but Morli had straightened his shoulders and taken to exploring. Not handling Baxter's possessions, just looking. Baxter didn't know whether to credit Morli's royal background or just his unique personality for his aplomb in this weird situation.

Morli's tour had inevitably taken him into the kitchen, where he was fascinated by everything from the plastic teakettle to the refrigerator.

"Any particular kind of bread you want me to make?" Baxter asked.

"Your favorite."

Baxter had several favorites, but after considering, he opted for a cranberry oatmeal loaf that made incredible turkey sandwiches. Morli watched every move as Baxter gathered the ingredients. "These dried berries," he said, nibbling on one, "we don't have them. But they taste a bit like frostfruit. Do you have that?"

"I don't think so."

"We use it mostly for flavoring liquor. But I bet I could dry it and use it like these cranberries. I'll have to—" He broke off abruptly and, for a second, seemed defeated. But then he lifted his chin. "Show me the rest, please."

Baxter had invested in a KitchenAid mixer back in April, when it was becoming clear that California's sheltering in place was going to last for a while. The appliance took up a good chunk of counter real estate. But Morli got very excited over it, and that was fun to see. He also noted that aside from the yeast, the ingredients were similar to ones he was used to. "Our worlds aren't entirely different," he said with a grin. "I like knowing that bread is bread."

While they waited for the dough to rise, Baxter made sandwiches, which he served with potato chips. Morli had never had chips before and decided he liked them very much. "Salty," he said with approval. "And noisy. If we had these in my kingdom, my parents would ban them from the royal table for being undignified." He crunched loudly, displaying his opinion.

They were almost finished eating when Morli cocked his head. "Why are you alone here? Where's your family?"

Baxter realized he was making a face and tried to smooth his expression. "Aunt Opal died last year. She's the only one I was close to. My parents...." Ugh. How to explain without sounding whiny, especially to a guy whose own mother and father had sent him to his death. "I don't think they ever wanted a kid, and they never knew what to do with me. We're nothing alike. We never had much to say to one another."

"Maybe you're a changeling," Morli said with complete seriousness.

"I don't think we have those here. Plus, I look exactly like my dad." That had always been a puzzle—how could they resemble each other so closely on the outside and not at all on the inside? "Anyway, we don't hate each other. We talk a couple of times a year. On my birthday and Christmas. I don't have any other close relatives. And the ex-boyfriend and my few friends are back in Chicago. That's, um, really, really far away."

Morli didn't even flinch at the boyfriend part. In fact, he reached across the table to take one of Baxter's hands in both of his, which were pleasantly warm. "I'm sorry," he said. Which was ridiculous considering that he was the one with much bigger problems. But, man, it was nice to hear.

Baxter wondered why Morli hadn't freaked out over the boyfriend part. Maybe he didn't know what that meant in this world. Better to clarify it now instead of startling him later. Baxter had come out of the closet at fourteen—much to his parents' chagrin—and never intended to go back in. "My ex-boyfriend, his name was Sven. We dated for almost a year." If you could call it dating. Mostly they just got together and fucked. "Then we figured out we weren't very compatible except in bed."

"Probably better to decide that before you married."

"Yeah, probably. But it doesn't bother you that my lover was a man?"

Morli looked puzzled. "Why would that bother me?"

Baxter wanted to kick himself. Why had he assumed that Morli was a homophobe? "A lot of people don't think others should hook up with the same gender."

"Why not? If an heir is required, then I guess that makes sense, but that's usually not a worry outside the nobility." He made a sour face. "My parents talked about me wedding Princess Osenne, but I think they were mostly interested in her wealth. And station. That's why they intervened in my affair with the brewer. Colau. He was very good at his job, and I liked spending time with him. But he was a commoner and had no fortune. They sent him away."

So Morli liked men. They were still holding hands, and although there was nothing sexual about it, the touch suddenly felt more important. Baxter's skin tingled where it was in contact with Morli's.

He cleared his throat. "I'm sorry they did that. Here some people think it's immoral. Or that God disapproves."

Morli laughed. "The gods create love. Why in heavens would they disapprove?"

Baxter had no answer for that. He changed topics slightly by asking about religious practices in Morli's kingdom, which was interesting enough to keep them talking until the bread had to be punched down and shaped into loaves. Morli did that while Baxter watched and wondered why he'd never noticed before how sensual kneading could be.

THEY STAYED up very late that night, talking and eating. Baxter ordered pizza—another wonderful discovery for Morli—and they each drank a couple of beers. Morli was astonished at many of the things Baxter told him, and they found so many things to discuss that Baxter felt as if they could converse for years. Morli genuinely seemed to enjoy his company, and Baxter never once felt awkward or uncomfortable.

Of course, some things horrified Morli, such as learning about the pandemic and why ashes were falling from the sky, not to mention the current state of American politics. But he was also delighted by so much: Baxter's music, the concept of ebooks, YouTube videos of cats, central air conditioning, and Baxter's unnecessarily large yarn stash. He took great pains to try to understand Baxter's job.

"You make paintings so people will want to buy your vegetables?" His brows were earnestly drawn.

Baxter, who suspected that advertising was pretty rudimentary where Morli came from, tried to explain. "Joaquin Foods, the company I work for, sells canned vegetables and sauces. I'm a production artist. Sometimes I help with labels and brochures and stuff, but mostly I help create the materials for trade shows. Which is where the company's salesmen try to convince stores and restaurants to buy our products. I do the banners, the table signs, the swag. Things like that. Lately, since the pandemic's put trade shows on hold, I've been working on a bunch of things related to our website updates."

He was aware that Morli probably didn't know what most of that meant. Which was fine because it was all really boring anyway. Sven, who was a personal trainer, had waved his hand dismissively whenever Baxter mentioned his work.

Morli smiled though. "You're an artist. You're good at so many things!" Very flattering indeed. But then he tried to hide a yawn and failed.

"God, you must be exhausted," Baxter said. "And I have to get up early for work. Want to call it a night?"

"Not really. There's so much I want to talk to you about. But I suppose we ought to stop."

Baxter, who'd been sitting beside Morli, stood and looked down at the couch. It was comfortable enough for lounging, but he'd fallen asleep there a couple of times and awakened with a backache. Of course, Morli was shorter and might fit better. But Morli had been going through some hard shit and deserved as much relaxation as he could get. Baxter had only one bed and didn't want to sleep on the couch either. On the other hand, Morli was a guest and royalty, which meant he shouldn't be consigned to second-best. But—

"Are you all right, Baxter?" Morli looked worried.

"Do you want to share my bed tonight?"

"You wouldn't mind?"

That wasn't the response Baxter had expected. "No, it'll be fine. It's a California King. Which is kinda big for one person, except I'm tall so I appreciate the leg room." That was more detail than Morli likely wanted. Baxter took a breath. "Plenty of space."

"Thank you," Morli said with a big grin.

Getting ready for bed was easy enough. Morli had already mastered modern plumbing, and Baxter had given him a new toothbrush and comb. But in the bedroom Baxter discovered that Morli slept naked and was unselfconscious about his nudity. That made sense in the warm weather, and Baxter had already seen him without clothes. But that was before Baxter knew that Morli was into guys and before he'd spent an entire day hanging out and enjoying his company. Also, it was really hard to not stare at the cupcake tattoo.

Baxter kept his underwear on—boring, conservative boxers—and was grateful when Morli got under the blanket. Well, until he experienced Morli's delicious scent and the knowledge that the beautiful bare body was inches away.

"Baxter?" Morli's voice was a whisper in the darkness.

"Hmm?"

"The spell your Aunt Opal gave you. What was it for?"

"Happiness," Baxter whispered back. Then he rolled away from Morli and tried to sleep.

8

———————

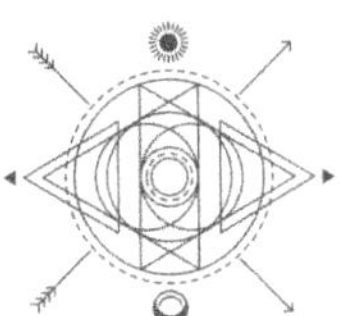

Morli couldn't sleep. The bed wasn't the problem; it was by far the most comfortable he'd ever encountered, and the sheets were so soft and smooth. Just a few additional miracles of Baxter's world.

Although a great many shocking things had happened to Morli in the past two days, they weren't keeping him awake either. Generally, his strategy when dealing with adversity was to pull the covers over his head and hibernate for as long as possible, which rarely solved anything but at least let him escape for a while.

And although his future was one enormous mystery, he wasn't frightened by the uncertainty. At least he seemed to have some kind of future—which was more than he'd expected while trudging toward the tower—and he was certainly having a very exciting adventure. More importantly, though, Baxter had found him, and Baxter was a kind and generous man. Morli had faith that Baxter wouldn't abandon him to some terrible fate.

It was Baxter, actually, who was keeping him awake. Not

on purpose. In fact, Baxter's long body was curled away from Morli, his breaths coming deep and slow. Morli was awake with thoughts of what an astonishing man Baxter was.

Very few people in Morli's world—or, he suspected, in Baxter's—would have responded to Morli's sudden and strange arrival by bringing him into their home and giving him clothing, food, comfort, and a place to sleep, patiently explaining all the new things, and appearing genuinely interested in what Morli said. Yet Baxter had done all of those things and more. He asked for nothing in return. And he was sweet and funny and not at all full of himself. He didn't act as if there was anything unusual about Morli, even though there most definitely was. There was also a sadness to Baxter that Morli understood completely: Baxter existed in his world all alone.

What Morli truly wanted was to snuggle up against Baxter and see if Baxter would welcome his caresses. But surely Baxter wouldn't. Morli was... an aberration. Not truly human, he was instead a monster made of food scraps. He was fortunate that Baxter had been treating him with such courtesy, but surely that could only extend so far. Who'd want to make love with a... thing?

Instead of pining over what he couldn't have—and by moving very slowly so as not to disturb Baxter—Morli slipped out of bed and padded to the bathroom. That small space was full of wonders, but he wanted the mirror just now.

Morli's family had experienced some difficulty with mirrors. His great-great-great-grandmother, Queen Hamnita the Vain, had owned an enchanted looking glass that, when asked, told her a bold-faced lie: that she was the loveliest woman in the land. Hamnita treasured the looking glass, despite the fact that it caused some type of extreme unpleasantness involving one of her stepdaughters. The details had been largely erased from the official histories. The glass itself was ultimately shattered, and shards of it now reposed within a case in the great hall, serving as either a genealogical souvenir or a life lesson, depending on whom you asked.

Mercifully, Baxter's mirror didn't speak. It simply cast a reflection, showing him a stranger's face. Objectively, the face was handsomer than his own, which had been too narrow with thin lips and a too-long chin. He traced fingertips over the green eyebrows, the straight-bridged nose, the full lips. Yes, not bad at all if you could overlook the coloring of his hair and eyes. Maybe he'd get used to it in time, along with the unfamiliar feel of this body, which had different proportions than his previous one. He was slightly taller now, with wiry muscles like the gymnasts who sometimes performed for the court. Before he'd been bony and had a small potbelly.

He looked down at his dick. It was different too, girthier and nestled now in green curls instead of brown. He hadn't paid much attention to the length when he'd woken up hard that morning, so he didn't know how that compared.

Whatever force had gifted him with this body—the raven or the spell or the gods—had been generous, albeit with an apparent sense of humor. What if they'd made him out of something else, such as a mushroom or a tuft of moss? That might not have turned out so well. Although he was very grateful, he still mourned his old body, now rotting amid the bramble, and he missed his home. His... *self*.

"Are you okay?"

Startled, Morli jumped and spun around. Baxter stood

in the bathroom doorway with his hair mussed and a pillow mark on his cheek.

"I'm sorry," Morli said. "I didn't mean to wake you."

"You didn't. I forgot to turn off the sound on my phone and it made a noise. Someone I follow on Instagram has a new story."

Despite not knowing what that meant, Morli nodded. "I'll get out of your way."

Baxter stepped out of the doorway to let him pass but stopped Morli by putting a hand on his shoulder. "Is something wrong? Do you need anything?"

Morli didn't know whether it was the concern in Baxter's voice or the sympathy in his touch, but Morli's chest hitched and his throat caught, and then he began to cry. Not quiet noble tears, but rather loud tearing sobs that hurt his lungs and made his nose run. He hadn't cried like that since he was a child, and even then his governess had told him to stop sniveling and act like a prince.

But Baxter didn't admonish him. In fact, he enfolded Morli into his arms and smoothed his hair, making quiet reassuring sounds. It felt wonderful to be comforted, but somehow it only made Morli cry harder. Baxter held him, infinitely patient.

By the time his wails had turned to sniffles, Morli was hollowed out. "Sorry," he said, reluctantly pulling away.

"It's fine. I've had several good cries since the pandemic started. It's better than punching walls."

"It's not very"—Morli was going to say *princely*, but he wasn't one anymore—"mature."

"I don't know how it is where you come from, but lots of people here say that crying isn't manly. Aunt Opal used to encourage me, though. She said it's cathartic. Flushes out the toxins." He grinned a little. "She used to watch a really sappy, weepy movie once a week so she could have a good cry. Kleenex therapy, she called it."

Morli found himself smiling back. It was hard not to.

After Morli washed his face, he grabbed his borrowed trousers and met Baxter in the kitchen, where they drank some water and finished the muffins. They didn't really talk, but that was all right. It was nice just to have company.

Eventually they returned to the bedroom and climbed into bed. Not touching, but almost. Baxter turned out the light, and Morli fell asleep at once.

IN THE MORNING, Baxter showed Morli how to use the shower. It was spectacular. At home he'd bathed with a washbasin and towel, shivering violently if it was winter. He'd clean his hair outside, rubbing in some prickly-scented powders and then pouring cups of water over it to rinse. Sometimes he used the big copper vessel in the palace tub room, but that was an ordeal requiring a parade of servants heating buckets of water over a fire, and it rarely felt worth the effort. The shower, though, was like a warm waterfall, and Baxter's sweet-scented shampoo and soap made rich suds.

Baxter also gave him clean clothes—another pair of those strange baggy trousers and a loose shirt with the image of a green giant wearing torn blue hose—but he seemed apologetic. "We'll get you some clothing today," he promised, although Morli didn't mind the borrowed ones. They were soft and easy to put on and take off.

After that, Baxter demonstrated how to use the stove. He cooked them flat cakes that he called, appropriately enough, pancakes, and watched with amusement as Morli attempted to fry sausage. He'd never done that before, not even at home, where he'd been grudgingly allowed access to the ovens but not the cooking fires. The sausages turned out only a little burned. They ate the cakes smothered with butter and a sweet, sticky liquid called maple syrup. "What does the maple fruit look like?" Morli asked.

"I don't think a maple tree has fruit. The syrup comes from the tree sap."

Interesting. It was very tasty stuff, and as Morli helped wash dishes afterward—another first for him—he thought about how he might use the syrup as a sweetener in bread or cakes.

Then it was time for Baxter to go to work, which meant he went into the spare room and stared at the thing he called a computer, poking his fingers at the letters on an attached board. Morli thought about starting some bread but decided he wasn't yet comfortable enough in the kitchen. He might accidentally burn the place down.

After meandering through the house for a time, picking things up and putting them down, wondering what they were for, Morli stood in front of a shelf full of books. This was an astounding thing to begin with, because in his world books were very expensive; even the palace contained only a handful. Baxter's were bound in paper instead of thick leather, and they had bright pictures on the covers. Baxter had told him that some were true accounts or explanations, while others contained stories.

He chose a book with two towers on the cover and curled up with it on the couch. It turned out these towers did not contain enchanted princesses, although an enchanted ring and some sorcerers were involved. He decided this was probably not one of the true accounts, and he enjoyed it quite a bit even if he didn't fully understand it.

He was also slightly envious of the fellow named Frodo because he had a true friend to accompany him on his quest instead of a disgruntled overaged squire.

Of course Frodo had his share of problems. But he was a true hero, brave despite reluctance and temptations. Not at all like Morli, who was... nothing.

His stomach growled. It was hard to tell the time with the sky pinkish-gray from the smoke, but he suspected it had been a long time since breakfast. After setting aside the book, he padded to Baxter's room and rapped softly on the door.

Baxter turned around with a smile. "Sorry. I've abandoned you."

"Would you like me to make you a sandwich?" He could manage that much without destroying the kitchen.

"I'd love that." Baxter's eyes gleamed with happiness. "I forget to eat sometimes when I get wrapped up in work."

"May I see what you're doing?"

Baxter shrugged and waved him toward the computer. The screen was glass and rather like an enchanted mirror, except according to Baxter it operated by technology rather than magic. Morli was beginning to believe those were two names for very much the same thing. In any case, now the screen showed an image of a glass bottle containing a dark-red substance and sporting arms, legs, and a face. It appeared to be waving. "What do you call these creatures?"

"Nothing. I mean, it's an advertising concept, not a real thing. We don't have sentient foods."

Morli gave him a long look.

Blushing, Baxter shook his head. "I don't think you're a food."

"But I'm made from food."

"And I'm ninety-eight percent water, but that doesn't mean I *am* water."

Although he didn't quite trust the analogy, Morli didn't want to argue. "I like your advertising concept."

"Does it make you want to buy barbecue sauce?"

"I don't know what that is, and I've never bought anything in my life," Morli said. "But yes?"

"Never bought anything?"

"Well, indirectly. I've ordered things to be purchased, but someone else shops and pays. A servant." He'd never given it much thought and had only vague concepts of the costs of things. Unlike his brothers, however, he didn't collect expensive clothing and jewelry and wine. For the most part, the only he thing he'd wanted was baking ingredients.

Baxter looked contemplative. "Tell you what. I've already accomplished a lot today, and I worked yesterday, so I'm ahead. Let's eat and then go shopping. You need clothes and stuff."

"You know I have no money."

"You were born two days ago, sort of," Baxter said with a wide grin. "I owe you a birthday present." He turned back to his computer and made the letter-board click-clack for a moment. The screen went blank and he hopped off his chair. "Lunch?"

Morli insisted on preparing the sandwiches while Baxter sat at the table. "I feel like I'm the royal one," Baxter said. "I can't remember the last time anyone made food for me except at a restaurant."

"Did your Aunt Opal cook for you?"

Baxter laughed. "Not if I could talk her out of it. She had a lot of recipes, but she was a disaster in the kitchen. Sometimes she'd experiment and combine things she should *not* have, sometimes she'd get distracted, sometimes she'd just choose weird-ass dishes and then make them worse with substitutions." His expression was soft and his eyes focused far away as if these were treasured memories.

Morli brought the plates to the table and sat across from him. "What about your lover? I'm sorry—I forgot his name. He didn't cook for you?"

"Sven?" Baxter snorted. "He lived off protein shakes. Besides, we didn't have that kind of relationship. Did you make things for Colau, or was that not allowed since you're a prince?"

Unaccountably pleased that Baxter had remembered Colau's name, Morli nodded. "It was disapproved of, but I did it anyway. He had a certain small cake that was his favorite. And of course he saved his best ales for me." That was a treasured memory too—getting up before dawn to bake and then meeting Colau in the buttery for a snack and... activities. Colau was several years older than Morli and considerably more experienced. He always had a lot of clever ideas for how they could spend their time together.

After lunch, Baxter searched for shoes for Morli, whose feet were smaller than his. He finally produced a very odd set of footwear he called flip-flops. It felt strange to have a strap between his toes and to have the sole slap against his feet, but at least they wouldn't give him blisters like the stupid boots he'd been wearing when he died. Thinking about those boots made him truly angry for the first time. His family had sent him to his death and all they'd cared about was what he'd looked like. They might at least have wanted him to be comfortable in his final hours.

Morli couldn't stew over this, however, because Baxter led him to his vehicle, showed him how to strap in, and then they rolled away. It was terrifying and exhilarating all at once to travel so fast. Morli couldn't even concentrate on the scenery—he was too busy clutching the seat and wondering if he was about to die again. Aside from its speed, this vehicle was a little like a carriage, but with nothing pulling it. Baxter said it was called a car and was powered by something called an internal combustion engine, which Morli thought was likely another form of magic.

Eventually they stopped in a place filled with tidy rows of cars. The adjacent long, low building sported several signs, most of which meant nothing to Morli, but Baxter had parked closest to something that resembled a huge stylized target. Nobody would have any problem hitting that thing with their arrows.

Baxter handed him a piece of fabric. "We have to wear masks. Also try to stay at least six feet away from other people and—um, do you know how far that is?"

Morli shook his head.

"I'm a little over six feet tall. So if I could lie down and fit between you and the other guy, we're good. And try not to touch too many things. I have hand sanitizer for when we're done." He pointed to a small bottle filled with clear gel.

"This is due to your plague?"

"Yeah. And it sucks. We've all had to make a lot of changes really fast, and some people think it's more important to feel free than to protect others. Hundreds of thousands of people have died."

"We had a plague," Morli said. "A few years before I was born. I don't remember it, of course, but I've read accounts. It was called The Fade."

Baxter, who had been about to open his door, paused. "The Fade?"

"Yes. Many people who caught it became only a little ill. They lost their appetites and felt light-headed for a few days, and then they were fine. But others just got worse. All the colors gradually disappeared from their bodies, and then their bodies became transparent. Eventually...." He moved his hands in a *poof* motion. "The accounts said it wasn't painful. The afflicted simply grew less and less there and then they vanished. My parents lost a child to The Fade, a daughter. I think they were disappointed when I was not born a girl. They'd had enough sons."

He'd never said that last part aloud, and in fact, he'd never fully admitted it to himself. But it did help explain his unpopularity among his family. They'd wanted a replacement princess and had gotten him instead. A disappointment from the start.

Baxter set a hand on Morli's arm. "I'm sorry about your sister. And I'm also sorry your parents didn't realize how wonderful you are."

Morli watched Baxter put on his mask and then donned his own. He turned to face Baxter, wondering if he could tell he was attempting to smile. "Show me what it's like to shop."

"Shopping used to be different here. We didn't have to worry about social distancing and masks and stuff. And we could browse to our hearts' content. Today we're going to be task-oriented and efficient." Baxter heaved a heavy sigh.

The store was enormous. That was the first thing Morli noticed: a vast space possibly bigger than the palace, filled with shelf after shelf of objects. It made him realize how small his kingdom was compared to Baxter's home. The lights were bright and the colors garish, and he didn't recognize most of the items he saw. He would have been completely overwhelmed if not for Baxter's big, calm presence beside him.

"These aren't exactly royal luxuries," Baxter said. "But we'll find pretty much everything you might need. We can get you fancier things later if you want."

Morli didn't need anything fancy. He watched Baxter fetch a wheeled cart and then followed him deeper into the store. They began with clothing. Baxter had to explain what various things were for. Remembering what Baxter had said about moving quickly, Morli chose a few shirts and trousers, some strange stockings that covered only the feet and ankles, and small scraps of cloth that Baxter called underwear. After that, he looked at shoes and settled on a screamingly red pair with laces.

"Those are great," Baxter said. "You could find your feet in the fog."

Morli hesitated. "My parents would hate them. Undignified."

"Your parents aren't here. Suit *yourself.*"

Grinning, Morli dropped them into the cart.

As they sped along, Morli glanced down endless aisles containing more things than he'd ever imagined. If ordinary people had so much, then the kings and queens here must be well stocked indeed. Oh, he'd forgotten. No royalty here. But Baxter said they had celebrities and zillionaires, which were almost the same thing.

Baxter helped Morli find other things as well, such as a hairbrush and a razor, and encouraged him to pick out a few books. Although Baxter gave information or advice when asked, he never criticized Morli's choices or made him feel foolish.

Morli could easily have gotten carried away in the cookware section, which contained such a tempting array of pans and other wares. He was mindful of the costs, however, and the limited space in Baxter's kitchen. Even though Baxter encouraged him to get more, Morli selected only one item. "This will make cakes shaped like mountains. Very clever."

And still they weren't finished. Another section of the store had lots of things colored orange and black. They were decorations for a holiday called Halloween, Baxter explained. "Aunt Opal loved Halloween. She'd buy the kitschiest witches she could find and help me cut bats and ghosts and pumpkins out of construction paper."

"What's this?" Morli pointed to an arched gray shape made of thick paper. It said Rest in Pieces.

"Tombstone. For fun, not for a real grave."

"I don't have a grave," Morli said thoughtfully.

Baxter looked chagrined. "Oh god, I'm being insensitive. I'm sorry—I didn't think. We can leave this section."

But Morli thought a holiday celebrating the dead was sweet. He put a hand on Baxter's arm to reassure him. "It's fine. And look at that." He indicated a mask intended to resemble a raven's head.

Their final stop was a section with food, most of which Morli didn't recognize. Everything was in boxes, bags, bottles, or other containers with enticing images and mystifying names. Baxter got some sugar, flour, and butter—at least Morli knew what those were—along with something called ice cream. "I think you're gonna love this."

Morli gazed at the full cart. "This will be very expensive."

"I'm good for it."

"But—"

"I make a decent salary. And I've saved a fortune by doing my own cooking for the past six months. I can afford this and I want to do it. I like giving gifts. Please."

"Thank you." Morli felt full of gratitude for this kind man.

They had a great many bags to carry out. As they

wheeled them to the car, they spied a large black bird perched on the top, its beak open as if it were smiling.

"You know, I googled ravens," Baxter said. "They're not supposed to live around here. We have crows, but they're smaller." The bird bobbed its head and made a sound like rough laughter. "Is that your raven?"

"I don't know." Morli walked closer to the car. "Are you the raven who ate my eyes?" he called. A middle-aged woman nearby gave him a frightened look and got quickly into her car, but the raven didn't answer. Morli shrugged. "Follow us back to Baxter's house and I'll feed you."

The raven croaked and flapped heavily away.

"You're not going to give it your eyes again, are you?" Baxter asked as they drove off.

"Not while I'm still using them. Do you suppose they taste like vegetables?"

Baxter turned his head briefly, looking appalled. "That's awful."

"I guess." But Morli was actually happy the raven had snacked on him. At least he'd been of some use, even if he had to die to accomplish it. He thought about the princess, asleep in her tower, and what she'd think when she woke up —*if* she woke up—and saw all those ragged corpses hanging from the bramble. Maybe she'd feel responsible, even though it wasn't her fault. Or maybe she wouldn't care. If any of Morli's brothers were enchanted, they wouldn't spare any thought at all for those who'd perished trying to save them. They'd just figure it was their due.

Back at Baxter's house, they had lots of things to put away. Baxter cleared a dresser drawer for Morli's new clothing, then cut off the tags and threw the garments in the washing machine. Morli spent several fascinated minutes watching the fabric tumble around inside the contraption.

Then they gathered some scraps from the kitchen, including leftover bread crusts—one of which Baxter spread with an odd substance called peanut butter—and a partial bag of unsalted sunflower seeds. They set the food on a patch of grass near some of Baxter's vegetable plants and backed away to the door. Neither of them was surprised when the raven swooped down and began to eat.

"Thank you," Morli said to her. "For bringing me on this adventure. It's wonderful."

She croaked softly at him, her mouth full of bread.

Baxter shifted on his feet and cleared his throat a few times. "Um, thank you? I don't know whether you chose me on purpose for this or if mine was just a random house with sourdough starter outside. But I'm really glad Morli's here."

He was telling the truth, Morli realized. For maybe the first time ever, someone was grateful for his presence. That knowledge warmed his heart as if it were an oven, and he wrapped his arms around himself to hold in the happiness.

"We should probably go in," Baxter said after a few minutes. "The AQI is, like, 180."

Morli furrowed his brow. "AQI?"

"The air quality index."

For a few moments, Morli wondered whether it applied to the smoke in the air or to the plague. Baxter's world had so many dangers to worry about! They went back into the house and Baxter hovered near the couch. "I, uh... need to work. Are you okay if I...." He gestured vaguely toward the spare room.

Morli picked up the book he'd begun. "I can entertain myself."

Baxter gave a nod and left the living room. But a very short time later, he wandered back out and collapsed next to Morli on the couch. "Can't concentrate. I've accomplished enough already today; the color range on Mr. Saucy is much better."

"Mr. Saucy?"

"Yeah. But," he hastened to add, "I didn't name him. I mean, okay, there's a pun in the name that they're going to play up in the advertising campaign, but I think it's derivative of Mr. Peanut."

He leaned over and picked up an oddly shaped black item. Like many items in this world, it was made of plastic and had buttons to push, but Morli couldn't discern its purpose. Then the big glass screen lit up and an image appeared. It was a village that somewhat reminded him of his kingdom.

"Where is that?" Morli set down the book.

Baxter was doing something to the plastic device with his fingers. "Nowhere. I mean, it's not real. It's a game."

"A game?"

"Yeah. See, I'm an orc named Retxab, which I know isn't very clever, but I spent way too long deciding what my character looked like, and I didn't want to fuss over the name. I'm on a quest. I control what my character does. Like... shit!" He moved the plastic thing quite violently. At the same time, the person on the screen began running, chased by two men with swords. The orc tripped, rolled over, and began to fight with the men. He ended up killing them both.

Baxter turned to him and grinned. "I didn't die that time."

"You can die?" Morli tensed with alarm.

"Not for real. My character can. Then I have to start again."

Morli relaxed. "Oh. So it's like a story, but on a screen."

"Exactly."

Morli continued watching. Baxter's character didn't just get into fights. Sometimes he talked to people or walked through a forest. Sometimes he stole things. It was interesting, and Baxter acted almost as if the action were real, swearing when things went wrong and celebrating when he had a success.

Morli smiled when a dragon landed in front of Baxter's orc. But then the orc began to swing his blade, and Morli watched in horror as the dragon was slain. "Yes!" Baxter said.

"You can't kill a dragon! That's terrible."

Baxter's eyebrows rose. "Oh? Why?"

"They're very rare. And if they die out, who will guard the borders?" Since Baxter looked mystified, Morli explained. "It's how peace has been maintained—well, mostly—between the kingdoms for generations. Nobody's going to send an army if there's a dragon. My family employs seven, which is enough to make our neighbors a little envious. I've met a few of the creatures. They're very nice."

"You have... dragons. Real ones."

"We won't if people go around killing them."

Morli was aware he sounded affronted, but this was an important matter. Before kingdoms had employed dragons, they were constantly waging war and untold numbers of people had been killed. Besides, Udrodia's dragons were renowned for their charm and courtesy. Tourists came just to see them, which was good for the shops and inns near the borders. And one of his favorites—a shiny green dragon named Zyrsis—always chatted with the traders, and if they had unusual grains or sweeteners, she recommended they stop at the palace and ask for Prince Morli.

"Your world must be amazing," Baxter said a little

dreamily. "Real dragons! And magic. And, evidently, talking ravens."

"You have cars and Target and computers and Kitchen-Aids," Morli pointed out. "And pizza. I'm definitely going to learn to make that so I can—" He stopped so suddenly that he nearly bit his tongue.

Baxter gave him a kind look. "How about if I play Fallout instead? There are no dragons in Fallout."

They spent the rest of the afternoon together on the couch, Baxter playing and Morli reading, and then worked together to prepare dinner. They had something called spaghetti, served with salad and warm bread, and it was all very good. After washing up, they returned to the couch. Baxter turned on some music—strange to Morli's ears, but he liked it—and they sat together with their separate pursuits.

Not for the first time since he'd arrived, Morli admired the comfort of Baxter's furniture, which was far superior to anything in the palace. He also liked the coziness of Baxter's home and the quiet way Baxter inhabited it. For such a big man, he didn't take up too much space. Unlike Morli's relatives, he never stomped and shouted, as if the entire world ought to jump at his pleasure. And he smiled a lot, sometimes for no reason Morli could discern. Just quick flashes of sunshine that Morli couldn't help but return.

Morli had never felt so comfortable in anyone's company. He felt as if he could be entirely himself, which was ironic since he was *not* himself but rather a dead man inhabiting a constructed body. Baxter had no expectations of him other than his help with some chores, and that was a nice change too. To be valued for who he was and not for what he did—or didn't—do.

They went to bed together. Morli wondered if wearing

underclothes to bed was a local custom. If so, it was a strange one. Morli had always slept naked in warm weather, donning nightclothes only when it got very cold. Morli was very aware of Baxter sleeping so close to him. He fell asleep longing to touch.

9

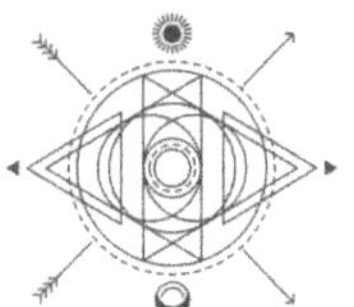

The air quality barely improved over the next week, much to Baxter's displeasure. "I'm missing my runs," he grumbled. Apparently he ran for pleasure and exercise, which Morli thought an odd concept. But then, he had swung a sword around, which he gathered was a rare pursuit in Modesto.

Baxter had to work, of course, so Morli spent that time baking and reading. But when Baxter's work was done, he'd take Morli for car rides, which were now only moderately terrifying. Morli could barely grasp the enormity of this place, the thousands and thousands of people it contained. Yet Baxter said Modesto was a small city. He showed Morli pictures and videos of big cities: New York, Tokyo, Delhi, Sao Paolo, Cairo. Those images took Morli's breath away. He imagined that if he were sent to one of those places, he'd cower in a corner somewhere, too scared to move.

From those images and from his discussion with Baxter, he learned that a great many people in this world were desperately poor. Starving, even. A few others, on the other hand, were wealthy beyond the dreams of any king or queen. "My kingdom too," he admitted. "I never went hungry or worried about where I'd sleep. I had servants to make my life easy in every way. My parents and my brothers would sometimes spend a fortune on a single article of clothing, wear it once, and then discard it. But peasants work hard their whole lives and have almost nothing. If there's a drought or a flood, if they get injured and can't work, some of them die." He'd tried to discuss this with his family a few times. Surely there must be some way to help the poor. Surely the royal family had so much that it could afford to give things up. But his parents refused to talk about it. Unseemly, they said. His brother Algar whispered the word *treason*.

It made Morli sad that this world, despite its many wonders, did no better.

But among the good things were countless new foods, more books with stories, and TV shows—especially the ones Baxter called Disney animation and the ones where people suddenly burst into song. "I heard about a sorcerer who was hired to provide magic lights for a wedding. But when the couple wouldn't pay, the sorcerer cursed the entire town. No more music. Not even humming."

"Your sorcerers like to curse, don't they?"

"Only when they're provoked." Morli frowned. "I don't know what Princess Osenne's family did. I imagine something awful." People didn't seem to tell that part of the story. The princess's parents had no doubt made sure their responsibility was edited out of all accounts.

Morli and Baxter fell into a long discussion about what constituted justice and who should decide it. Baxter had some very odd ideas, but it was enjoyable to discuss them even when they disagreed. He waved his arms around a lot when he became passionate about a point. Sometimes he knocked things over.

Demons' doorknobs, Morli wanted to touch him. Kiss him. Explore that big body.

But he didn't have the courage to try.

And then one evening they were talking about education. Morli had been given governesses and tutors, of course, whereas Baxter went to schools with other children. "I got pretty good grades," he said. "Not spectacular, but decent. My teachers learned they didn't have to put much effort into me in order for me to pass, but none of them expected anything spectacular from me either. I was sort of a ghost. My parents didn't care, as long as I didn't flunk or get into trouble. Aunt Opal, though, she'd shake her head at me. Tell me I could do better. 'Find your passion,' she said."

"Did that work?"

"Dunno. I never found it."

Morli tilted his head, trying to understand. "You have a job, though. I take it you do well at it."

"Sure. And don't get me wrong—my job's cool. Pays well. But it's hard to get passionate about Mr. Saucy." Baxter looked down at his big hands, fingers laced in his lap. His hair fell forward, obscuring his eyes, and his shoulders were hunched. It was as if he were making himself smaller. Invisible.

Morli scooted a little closer on the couch. "Do you have any idea what you might love?"

"No," Baxter said with a sigh. "I've taken online personality tests, but they didn't help. I thought maybe with some extra time on my hands during the pandemic I might find something. Knitting, gardening, baking... they're all fun. But they don't make me swoon."

"Did you have dreams once?"

A shake of the head. "No. My parents were so cold—maybe I never developed that spark. As a kid, I spent a lot of time with my nose in books. And I watched a lot of movies. Geeky stuff. Escapist, my parents said. Childish, Sven said. Science fiction and fantasy." He lifted his head with a tiny smile. "Stuff with dragons and princes and sorcerers. You have a passion, though."

For one sharp, spine-tingling moment, Morli thought Baxter was going to say, *Your passion is me.* But what he said instead was "Baking."

Ignoring the twinge of disappointment, Morli nodded. "When I was a boy, I'd sneak into the kitchens whenever I could. Maybe at first I was just looking for snacks, but pretty soon I grew fascinated with the bakers. They do so much with such simple ingredients. It's like a special kind of magic, with the magician so intimately involved. Choosing the recipe and the components. Measuring. Kneading the dough." He realized he was reflexively moving his fingers, and he set his hands on his knees to stop them.

"I get it," Baxter said. "It's rewarding too."

"Right! You feed people something wonderful. And even if you make a mistake, it's not a disaster. You just try again." Now his fingers were kneading his knees. "Baking is a *good* thing. A generous thing. Doing it well takes practice and skill and patience, and... and even some inborn talent, maybe. Baking is important. It's worthy." He remembered the derisive words of his parents and brothers, the sneers of the courtiers, even the scornful expressions of the servants when they didn't think he'd notice.

And once again he was sobbing, as if he had one of Baxter's light switches inside him, causing tears instead of light. He didn't want to do this; it was embarrassing and pointless. And stupid as well, because what did it matter what those people thought of him? He'd never see them again.

That thought only made him wail louder.

As before, Baxter gathered him into his arms. It was an awkward position, each of them twisted toward the other, Morli's face buried in Baxter's chest. Baxter couldn't possibly be comfortable, yet he hadn't hesitated in the embrace, and he kept his grip exactly firm enough to be comforting, never complaining or seeming to worry about the mess Morli was making on his shirt.

Morli remained in the hug longer than necessary, partly because he was too humiliated to face Baxter and partly because it simply felt good. But eventually he had to move. He wiggled his shoulders slightly and leaned back, and Baxter released him at once.

"I am so sorry," he said miserably.

"Don't be."

"I never used to cry. Really."

Baxter handed him a box of tissues from the side table. "I told you Aunt Opal's thoughts on the matter."

"But I'm not Aunt Opal! I'm a prin—" No, he wasn't. Not any longer. He was nothing. He blew his nose.

Baxter was silent for a long time before clearing his throat. "Aunt Opal died last June. It wasn't awful or anything. She'd just turned ninety-five, and I'd taken her out for a birthday dinner at the kind of restaurant where you have to make reservations months in advance. Very fancy. We dressed up and had a great time. And over dessert, she told me that she was done with life. 'It's time to blow this popsicle stand,' were her exact words. A couple of days later she died in her sleep." He sighed deeply.

Morli put a hand on Baxter's knee. "I'm so sorry."

"Thanks. She had a good run. She was a happy person,

you know? She used to laugh a lot. Anyway, after she died, I had a hard time getting over it. About three months later, I was still feeling it."

"Three months isn't long to grieve someone you love."

"One afternoon Sven came over to my place. We were supposed to work out together and then have sex. It was our routine. But I wasn't feeling it that day. Something had reminded me of Aunt Opal and I was… feeling blue. When I tried to explain to Sven, I burst into tears." Baxter's expression hardened. "And he was an asshole about it. Said real men don't cry. Told me it was time to stop moping about some old lady who wasn't even my grandma."

Anger at a man he'd never met surged through Morli's veins. If Sven had been in the room, Morli would have challenged him to a duel. Or maybe just punched him in the nose—that would be quick and satisfying. "That's awful."

"Actually, it was a good thing. That's the day I stopped seeing him. At which point he became an even bigger asshole and spread all kinds of lies about me to our mutual friends." Baxter lifted his chin. "I'm glad I broke it off when I did."

"He's a villain for treating you so poorly. And a fool for not valuing a man like you."

Their faces were quite close as Morli said this, so Baxter had to lean in only a little bit when he kissed him.

Oh, Vadal's virtue, it was a *wonderful* kiss.

Baxter's lips were soft and carried a hint of sugar from the apple tart Morli had made that day. He was the type of kisser who threw himself into the act entirely, lacing his fingers in Morli's hair and moving his body closer yet not pushy about it. Morli could easily have broken away if he wanted to. Hah! An entire tribe of ogres couldn't have torn him free.

Morli clasped his hands behind Baxter's neck and parted his lips, granting Baxter entry and letting him set the pace. Baxter was in no hurry. He savored the kiss as he would a meal, and when he moaned deep in his throat, Morli's entire body lit with desire. He imagined sparks crackling around him and Baxter, both of them glowing like suns. He imagined the smoke finally clearing and the gods smiling down at them from the skies. He imagined a love affair bards would sing about for generations.

Baxter pulled back slightly but kept his hands on Morli's shoulders. He was panting and wild-eyed, and when he spoke, his voice was rough. "I didn't plan to do that."

"I'm glad you did."

They stared at each other. "We could do it again," Morli suggested.

Baxter groaned. "If we did, I'd have a hard time stopping."

"I don't see why you should stop." Morli batted his eyelashes shamelessly. He'd throw himself onto Baxter's lap if necessary.

But Baxter didn't flirt back. In fact, he looked sad. "I see lots of reasons."

Hurt, Morli moved away. He'd almost forgotten that he wasn't real, that he was merely a construct of magic and refuse. That was stupid of him.

But Baxter gently took his hand. "I don't want.... You're the single most remarkable person I've ever met. I love hanging out with you. I don't want to fuck that up with, um, fucking. Especially when everything's new to you. God, what if you have Stockholm syndrome or something?"

Morli looked alarmed. "Is that another plague?"

Baxter barked a humorless laugh. "No. It's when a prisoner forms an emotional bond with their captor as a way of protecting themself from harm."

"I am not your captive. You didn't bring me here, and you've never stopped me from leaving." Morli pointed at the front door. "I could walk out at any time."

"And go where?"

Morli had no reasonable answer for that.

Baxter released Morli's hand and stood. "I'm a mess, okay? I've never had a meaningful romantic relationship with anyone. I'm lonely as hell. And you're so... so... incredible. But vulnerable too. And God, Morli, I'd never forgive myself if I hurt you."

The worst part was that Morli knew Baxter was right, which caused Morli to be both admiring of his character and angry at his decision. Together with the lust still simmering in his belly, the sadness remaining from old memories, and the general haze of confusion that had been on him since he died, he felt overwhelmed. He stood too. "I think I'd like to go to bed." It was too early for it, but it was the only thing he could face right now.

Backing away, Baxter nodded. "Okay. I think I'll get ahead on some work. Mr. Saucy is waiting." He turned, went into the spare room, and quietly closed the door.

10

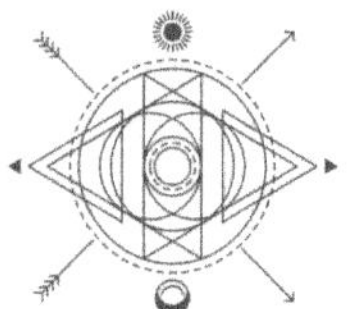

Morli got into bed but couldn't sleep. Every time he closed his eyes, he replayed that glorious kiss—and the disappointment that came after. He felt like a bird fluttering against its cage, imprisoned not by a cruel captor but by circumstances.

Baxter was right. Morli had nowhere to go in this world and was of no use to anyone. He didn't know the simplest acts of survival. Yet he realized now that he couldn't stay with Baxter. Not because Baxter would evict him—Morli was confident he'd do no such thing—but because Morli would be torturing them both. Without context and connections and a course of action, Morli would shrink into himself like an unrisen loaf. He'd slowly diminish, as if stricken with The Fade. He'd died once already and wasn't eager to do it again.

He found himself wishing he knew prayers for guidance, but he'd never learned any. Royalty was too lofty for that. Besides, he didn't know whether his gods could hear him in this world. They felt so far away.

"You should be grateful," he whispered to himself. And, in fact, he was. But he was also filled with sorrow.

Too many emotions. If they were ingredients in a dough, the bread would taste terrible.

Well, he had to do something. He couldn't simply haunt Baxter forever, brooding over what he couldn't have. And making Baxter miserable too, no doubt.

It was late when Baxter tiptoed into the bedroom wearing only his underclothes. "Oh," he said when he spied Morli sitting propped against the pillows. "You're still up." He hesitated for a moment and then got into bed, keeping as far as possible from Morli.

"I had a relative named Tazitto. Over three hundred years ago. Like me, he was a prince and a younger son. Unlike me, he was famous for his tracking skills. He fell in love with a beautiful woman, a commoner. Everyone disapproved. She didn't want him either—she was in love with a farrier and they were going to be married. But you know how princes are. Stubborn and spoiled and used to getting our way."

"You're not," Baxter protested.

Morli hushed him with a wave. "Tazitto kept wooing her and she kept refusing, which was dangerous considering their stations. Then one day Tazitto went out riding and, claiming his horse had gone lame, brought it to the farrier. After he retrieved the horse, he said that some coins were missing from his saddlebags. The farrier was tried for theft and hanged."

Even in the dimly lit room, Morli could see Baxter's wide eyes. "That's horrible."

"Yes. When the woman heard what had happened, she knew Tazitto would come for her next. She packed a few things and ran off into the Aksesh Forest. Even today it's huge and mostly untraveled by humans."

"But Tazitto was good at tracking. Like Prince Humperdinck."

"Yes." Morli didn't know who this Humperdinck was, but he was pleased with Baxter for identifying the problem.

"Did he find her?"

"Of course. He and his men caught up with her very quickly. He told her to come back with him; she refused. He *ordered* her to come—and she flew at him with a knife."

Baxter seemed as caught up in the tale as if he were a child. "Ooh, good for her! Did she get him?"

"She drew blood, yes. But she was a weaver, and he was a prince who'd been trained in combat. He grabbed the knife away and, enraged, slit her throat. She died gasping a curse: choketree. Do you have that here?"

"I don't think so." Baxter was no longer in danger of falling off the mattress, having inadvertently scooted a little closer. But they still weren't touching.

"It's a vine. It wraps around trees and other plants and sucks out their sap, killing them. Nasty stuff. Sometimes it creeps out of the forest and into farmland, and then you have to burn it right away before it spreads."

"Choketree, killer brambles.... Your world has scary plants."

"Your trees are burning and making the air unsafe to breathe." Morli wasn't sure if that was a fair analogy, but he didn't want to give the impression that his world was any more lethal than this one.

Apparently conceding, Baxter asked, "So what happened to Tazitto?"

"What you might predict. Choketree vines rushed toward him, bound him, and killed him. His men fled, leaving both bodies where they lay. Later, a search party convened, but nobody was as good at tracking as Tazitto, and they never found them. I suppose they remain there still."

Baxter looked a little puzzled. "Was the woman a sorcerer?"

"No. But some people have a touch of magic talent running through them. In extreme situations they can sometimes accomplish quite a bit."

For a while, Baxter was quiet, seeming to think about the tale. His hair was messy, Morli suddenly noticed, as if he'd been running fingers through it.

"Not that I don't appreciate a gory fairy tale now and then, but I'm guessing there's a reason you told me this one."

"Not really," Morli admitted. "I just happened to recall it. Perhaps I needed to remember what terrible choices some of my family have made." His sigh felt as if it came from the depths of his soul.

"Am I a terrible choice?"

"No. And I want to keep it that way." Morli shifted to sit more upright. "I can't stay here."

"But—"

"I *can't*. It's not that I want to leave you—much the opposite, in fact. But you were right. I'm too vulnerable. I've allowed myself to get tossed around by fate and other people's demands. I need to make my own path, Baxter. At least for a while." He looked down at the bedding to avoid eye contact, and he held his breath, hoping Baxter would understand.

"Where will you go?" Baxter whispered.

Morli sagged with relief. Baxter *did* understand. "I don't know. But I'll find my way somehow." He said that with more confidence than he felt.

"Will you— Please. At least let me give you some money. And a phone. You can be on my cell plan, and that way you can access information wherever you are. Or call to let me know you're all right."

"Thank you." Morli wasn't so prideful that he'd refuse all help.

"Maybe wait a while before you leave? Give yourself time to learn about what's out there and make a plan."

Morli looked him straight in the eyes. He wanted to stay, he truly did. Which is why he had to refuse. "If I don't leave now, it'll just get harder."

Baxter's mouth worked, but he nodded.

Because saying anything else would hurt too much, Morli lay down, rearranged his pillow, and rolled to face away from Baxter. The lights went out a few seconds later. He breathed in and out slowly and warned himself that he'd smack his head into the wall if more tears came. He'd cried enough as it was. Besides, if Baxter took him into his arms again, Morli might never come out.

He was dreaming of vines when Baxter shook him wake. "Morli? I thought of something." Baxter's voice was hoarse with urgency.

Morli struggled to wipe the sleep from his brain. He sat up and squinted at Baxter, but the room was too dark to discern any details. "Wha'?" He'd never been a quick riser, especially when nestled in a warm and comfortable bed.

"I have two more feathers."

That made no sense at all to Morli, who wondered if he was still dreaming. It seemed to be the sort of thing people said in dreams—phrases that were understandable but didn't mean anything. With ravens in his life lately, it was no wonder there were feathers on his mind.

"Two more feathers," Baxter repeated more slowly. "The

magic feathers. One of them brought you here, but I still have two more."

Oh, all right. "What will you do with them?" he asked through a yawn. He had no idea what the possibilities were, and he doubted whether Baxter did either.

"Send you home."

Suddenly Morli was entirely awake, his eyes wide in the darkness and his back rigid. "H-home?"

"If you want to go, that is."

"Will that work?"

"I don't know. It seems like it should, though. I mean, maybe we need to get the raven on board too, but at least we can try."

Morli was breathing so fast that he felt dizzy. It had never occurred to him that a return might be possible, but now that the possibility had been raised, it glowed in front of him like a jewel. Baxter's world was… fascinating. Shocking. Overwhelming. And it contained Baxter himself, which was a major benefit. But Morli didn't belong here. He yearned for the familiar twin moons, the quiet clomp of horses on dirt roads, the customs and scents that he'd known since birth.

"Yes. Please," he said.

"In the morning?"

"All right." That seemed to be a very long time away, and yet far too soon. Gods, he'd miss Baxter so badly! He knew that he'd never again meet anyone like him, and he doubted he'd ever find a friend who eased his soul the way Baxter did. But demons' doorknobs, he couldn't be in two places at once!

"Um, Morli? What if you go back and, um, your body doesn't?"

That was a fair question. Morli might return to his world

only to find himself an ethereal spirit—a ghost, he supposed. Or he might end up simply and finally dead. But he could end up in this body or another, given a second chance at life.

"Oh." A realization landed on him like a boulder.

"What?"

"Princess Osenne."

"What about her?"

"She likely still needs rescuing."

"You're not going to do that again?" Baxter sounded horrified.

Morli searched inside himself. "I probably will."

"But you died last time! There's the briar, and—"

"And a girl lies trapped, dreaming her life away."

Baxter didn't say anything right away, but Morli heard the soft scritch as he rubbed at his scalp, which he did sometimes when he was confused or lost in thought. When he concentrated hard on his work or a video game or cooking, the tip of his tongue stuck out slightly. When he was worried, he pulled at an ear. And when he was happy, his eyes sparkled and he threw back his head when he laughed.

"Morli," Baxter began. He stopped. Bounced his leg on the mattress. "Morli, if you die again, she'll *still* be trapped. And you'll be dead. Unless you expect another resurrection miracle from the raven."

"I don't." Morli had the strong suspicion that it had been a one-time thing. Strong magic like that wasn't usually repeated. "But if I don't try, I think I might end up hating myself."

"You're a hero already."

"Not really. I went to the tower last time because my family forced me to. This time it would be my choice. Do you see the difference?"

Baxter's answer was barely audible. "Yeah. I guess I do."

"Look, I won't just go rushing in this time. I couldn't even if I wanted to, since I no longer have a sword. I'll take my time. Develop a plan." He wasn't particularly optimistic he'd come up with a good plan, but he'd try.

"Maybe... maybe you can take something with you. Something that will get rid of the bramble."

"Like what?"

Baxter sighed. "I have no idea. But we can sleep on it."

They both lay down again, but now Morli was wide awake and could tell that Baxter was too. He was physically so close, and soon and forever he'd be unimaginably far away. For however long Morli survived at home, be it seconds or decades, he'd cherish the memories of his amazing adventures in Modesto and, even more, of the man he'd known here.

Wouldn't it be better to have one memory more?

Morli rolled over and faced Baxter. All he could see was the shape of Baxter's head on the pillow.

"Something wrong?" Baxter asked.

"I'm going to regret it forever if I don't do this." Morli leaned over and kissed him.

This time Baxter tasted of minty toothpaste and smelled of the herbal facial cleanser he used every night. His cheeks were lightly bristled and his hair very soft, and to Morli's immense joy, Baxter grasped Morli's shoulders and pulled him closer. "I'd regret it too," he rasped when they broke the kiss.

"The objections you had before...."

"Hardly matter if this is our last night."

So Morli kissed him again—greedily, voraciously. And then Morli rested full-length atop Baxter, the two of them bucking and writhing hard enough to dislodge the blanket.

Not that it mattered. There was plenty of heat between them.

Baxter's hands wandered over Morli's body, squeezing and stroking here and there, while Morli gripped Baxter's hair with both hands. By the twin moons, Baxter felt glorious beneath him. Long and solid, heart beating fast against Morli's, deep moans rolling from his chest.

"It's... been... a long time for me," Baxter panted. "God, it's been a year."

Morli stretched and then rocked his hips. "And this is entirely new in this body. It's as if I'm a virgin."

That made Baxter groan. "That's.... This is going to be over very fast if you keep that up."

Even though Baxter probably couldn't see, Morli grinned wickedly. "Do what? This?" He thrust again, slowly and firmly, prolonging the contact between their hard lengths. "Or this?" He dropped his head to whisper in Baxter's ear. "You're the only one who's ever touched me. The only one I've kissed. All of this is new to this person I am, and tonight I belong entirely to you." He wasn't teasing —well, not more than a little. Those words were the complete truth.

"I—I've never had sex with royalty before." Baxter was smiling even as he arched under Morli, chasing more friction.

"And I've never had sex with a production artist."

"A first, and only, for both of us, I bet."

They stilled at that, Morli cupping Baxter's face and Baxter gripping Morli's ass. Because Baxter was right, this *was* a first and only. That made it precious beyond all accounting.

"What would you like to do with me?" Morli asked, because anything would please him.

"Everything."

"If only we had eternity. But since we don't, choose."

Baxter considered.

It was one of the things Morli liked about him, the way Baxter would chew over an idea carefully without leaping to conclusions or rejecting ideas outright. "I don't have rubbers," Baxter finally said. "That limits us a little."

"Rubbers?"

"Um, condoms."

Morli shook his head. "I don't know what you mean."

"You, um, roll one onto your dick before having sex with someone."

"Ah, a sheathskin." Morli had never used one himself, but he'd heard of them, certainly. His brothers bragged about how many of them they'd used during some of their wilder parties. "Demons' doorknobs, can men get pregnant here?"

Baxter burst into laughter that nearly dislodged him. "No. Not cis men anyway." He grew suddenly more sober. "Rubbers help keep diseases from transmitting."

"Like your plague?"

"A different plague. One that killed a lot of people. There are treatments for it now, but it's still something you don't want to transmit."

Morli shivered against him. For all its wonders, Baxter's world could be a terrible place, where even breathing or making love could prove fatal. "Do you have this illness? Because I don't see how I could."

"I don't think I do. But I don't want to take any chance of giving you the virus."

"Is that even possible? I'm not real."

Baxter clutched him hard. "You are the realest person I've ever met." His voice softened, and he licked a broad stripe along Morli's neck, making him shiver again but for very different reasons. "And you smell delicious."

"I do?"

"Like fresh-baked bread. All the time. It's kind of been driving me crazy." As if to demonstrate, he licked again and followed up with a gentle bite to Morli's neck.

Which is when Morli remembered how hungry he was, how needy for Baxter's touch. He swooped down for a kiss that stole Baxter's breath. Baxter responded by pushing down on Morli's butt, pressing them together so completely that even a spell couldn't have separated them.

They took their time, though. They tasted each other thoroughly and carefully, they mapped skin with fingers and tongues, they rocked and whispered and even laughed together until it was exactly enough and almost too much. Morli's climax felt as sweet and gripping as a vat of thirst-flower honey, and if he'd drowned in it, he would have been content.

Sweaty and boneless, they lay with limbs tangled. "That was magical," Baxter said.

And Morli had to agree.

11

The morning brought hints of blue sky between a scattering of clouds. "The smoke's clearing," Baxter announced, looking at his phone. "You'll be able to breathe more easily."

"Only until you leave."

That was the only reference they made to Morli's imminent departure. They took turns showering and shaving and brushing their teeth, and once dressed, they met in the kitchen for bacon and the sweet rolls Morli had made the night before. They had orange juice too. Morli's world didn't have oranges, at least not so far as he knew, but he'd come to enjoy the flavor.

They sat across the table from each other, eating silently. There was no discomfort in the quiet; it was pleasant to simply gaze at each other while enjoying a good meal. Morli smiled as he thought of the breads and cakes now in Baxter's freezer. They'd continue to feed Baxter for some time, which was a nice thing to know. He would remember that as he approached the tower.

"Thank you," Morli said as they washed dishes afterward. "For last night."

"I enjoyed it at least as much as you did."

That was a pleasant thought, and it made Morli smile. But there was more that he needed to say. "Thank you also for... everything. For sharing your home with me."

"Again, I enjoyed that too. Maybe more than you did, actually." Sigh. "Here you were, stuck with a nerd in a little house in Modesto. Not much excit—"

"Don't." Morli put a soapy hand on Baxter's arm. "I've never met anyone I'd rather spend time with. I've never needed much excitement; I'm a simple man." His family had also used that word to describe him, only they meant it as an insult. Morli, on the other hand, found no shame in simplicity. He could make a loaf of bread with nothing more than flour, water, salt, and a bit of time and effort. Nothing was simpler than that, and yet the outcome was life-sustaining and delicious.

"I'll never meet anyone like you again," Baxter said mournfully.

"No green hair and strange eyes?"

"No *you*. You'd be remarkable no matter what you looked like."

Morli considered dragging Baxter into the bedroom for another round of lovemaking, but he dismissed the idea. It would only make it harder to leave. Instead he dried his hands on a towel and took a final slow look around the kitchen. It was much smaller than the palace kitchens, of course, and rather crowded for two people, but he liked its coziness and the machines it contained. He liked thinking of Baxter puttering around in here, grating zucchinis and measuring sourdough starter, creating the elements that had given Morli life.

"I'm sorry I ruined your spell," he said.

"What? What spell?"

"The one from Aunt Opal—for happiness."

Baxter frowned at him. "But I *got* happiness. More than I dreamed of. I wish it had lasted longer, but God, Morli. I wouldn't have traded this time for anything."

"Nor I."

A few minutes later, Baxter produced a satchel he called a backpack, and he insisted that Morli stuff it with his new clothing, a couple of books, a few lemon muffins, and Baxter's sharpest knife. Morli didn't have a sword, and Baxter didn't want him completely unarmed. And then, with a sheepish grin, he handed Morli a plastic bottle.

"What's this?" Morli tried to read the label, but it was mostly worn off.

"Awful stuff, actually. I found it in the garage when I moved in and probably should've thrown it away. But maybe it'll help with the bramble. Probably can't hurt."

"Help how?"

"It's an herbicide. It kills weeds." He scrunched up his face. "It's pretty nasty poison, actually. I think it's been banned. Be careful with it."

Morli nodded solemnly, and after Baxter wrapped the bottle in a series of plastic bags, Morli stuffed it into the pack. No matter how toxic the stuff was, there wasn't much of it, and he couldn't imagine it would have much effect on the enormous bramble. But it was kind of Baxter to offer.

Baxter helped adjust the straps so the pack fit neatly across Morli's back. It was heavy, but he wasn't willing to give up any of the contents. Not because he expected to have much use for the items once he got back home, but because they were gifts from Baxter and therefore precious. "I'm ready."

"Are you sure—"

"Baxter."

A heavy sigh. "You're right." Baxter looked around the living room. "Maybe we should do this outside? That's where you appeared, and I don't know what happens if you try to, um, travel from inside a closed building."

That made sense. No reason to make things riskier than they already were. Morli watched as Baxter went into the spare room and returned with a yellow envelope. He carried it gingerly in both hands as if it might explode. They went out the back door into Baxter's garden, where zucchini plants sprawled and ripe tomatoes and peppers provided bright red contrast among all the greens. More clouds had gathered during breakfast, and although Baxter said rain was unlikely at this time of year, the air smelled a bit damp. A nice change from the prior bitter ashy odor.

To neither man's surprise, a raven perched atop the tree-house next door, looking down at them. "I'm going home," Morli called to her. "It's been a wonderful adventure, but I can't stay."

She croaked back, but Morli didn't know what it meant.

Baxter and Morli stared at each other. Morli's throat was tight. "Please don't... don't touch me. I couldn't endure it." He knew he'd clutch Baxter and never let go.

Seeming to understand, Baxter gave a slow nod. He held out the envelope. "Just take a feather. There are two left."

With considerable reluctance, as if something might bite, Morli reached inside. No fangs took hold of his flesh. Instead his fingertips brushed something that tickled, and he pulled out a single feather—black and surprisingly large but with no weight to it.

Baxter shook the remaining feather into place, carefully

folded the envelope to protect it, and tucked it into his rear pocket. He backed up a few steps. "Okay." His voice shook.

"Wh-what do I do with it?"

"Click your heels three times and say there's no place like home?"

"What?"

"Sorry." Baxter shook his head. "Stupid joke. I don't really know how to use them. The vampire said raven feathers are tricky and I should go with my gut."

Morli wasn't sure that taking advice from vampires was wise, but he didn't have any alternate plan. He gazed down at the feather, wishing it had instructions printed on it. "I'd like to return home, please," he said.

Nothing happened.

Morli took a deep breath and forced himself to concentrate. "What did you do to bring me here?" he asked Baxter.

"I don't know. That wasn't my plan. I just held the feather and wished for happiness. To go with the spell, right? The feather went poof and then you arrived."

Wish. All right. Morli spoke very clearly. "Feather, I wish to return home, please."

Once again there was no reaction, although a white butterfly flapped by and veered off to flutter among the vegetables. Morli looked over at the raven. "Will you take me home? Please? It's not that I'm ungrateful, but I don't belong here. And I need to try again to rescue the princess. You're welcome to my eyes when I fail."

"Morli!" Baxter moaned.

The raven, however, preened a wing, unimpressed.

Morli had another idea. He shrugged out of the backpack and began removing his clothes, which was slightly awkward while holding the feather. Baxter looked panicky. "What are you doing? The kids next door—"

"Maybe the clothes and other items can't pass between worlds. I was naked when you found me, right?"

With a dubious expression, Baxter nodded.

But when Morli tried again, standing as bare as when he arrived, there was again no result. "Maybe it's because I'm alive," he said thoughtfully. He eyed the backpack, where the large knife was tucked away. "If I were dead or at least dying—"

Baxter leaped forward and snatched the pack away. "No. Uh-uh. No way." He clutched the bag to his chest.

"I don't know what else to try!" Morli knew he sounded petulant, but he was on the verge of tears. He'd been so certain—*they'd* been so certain—that this would work. Magic was more limited here than at home, but it did have some strength, and the feather had made such good sense. Because that was one thing about magic: it stuck to its own rules of logic, even if few people besides sorcerers understood those rules.

Sorcerers!

"Baxter, your great aunt was a witch."

"Yeah, but she's dead now and can't help us. A Ouija board won't help either. I tried that."

"I didn't intend to call upon her help. It's only... I have no magic talents at all. Few people do, which is probably just as well, but my family is renowned for being particularly lacking in the abilities to sing, do math, or work enchantments. But not you!"

Baxter blinked a few times. "Me?"

"We already know you can do magic. You probably inherited the ability. It does run in families. Didn't your aunt tell you that?"

"I— Oh." As was his habit, he thought about the idea for

a few moments. "Okay. That makes sense, I guess. You want me to hold the feather and wish you back?"

"Yes! Please." Morli held out the feather, and Baxter took it gingerly. Up in the treehouse, the raven gave a loud croak. Morli hoped that meant she approved of this course of action.

Baxter set down the pack. "You might as well put your clothes on and take the backpack."

Morli still wasn't sure that the items would survive the transition between worlds; he wasn't sure that this *body* would make it. But it would definitely be preferable to arrive with some supplies, if possible, so he obeyed. He looked at Baxter. "I want to say so many things to you."

"Me too. Good luck, Morli. You really are a hero."

Baxter's hands were shaking. Morli saw it clearly even through the blur of his unshed tears. But Baxter's voice was clear enough when he spoke. "I'd like for Morli to be happy, so please send him home."

The feather turned so bright that it hurt to look at it, although it didn't seem to burn Baxter. Then the feather disappeared with an audible puff.

And just after that, Morli disappeared too.

At least, he imagined that's how it looked to Baxter. From Morli's perspective, the world went completely dark except for the afterimage of the feather, which seemed to float in front of him. When he reached for it, something invisible grabbed his wrist and pulled hard enough to jerk him forward and make him yelp. He felt as if he were bursting through a very thin but elastic layer of dough. Then glaring light almost blinded him, the pressure on his wrist went away, and he stumbled onto his hands and knees, barking a shin on something hard.

He opened his eyes to find himself on a ground strewn

with stones and decaying leaves. Trees towered far overhead, their wide canopies blocking much of the sun. The air smelled of growing things, especially the sharp bite of autumnflare, a rare but unmistakable herb he occasionally used as a flavoring. Too much of it caused stomach distress, but a light sprinkling added a unique taste to earthy breads.

He was home.

Tears started to fall and he let them, unsure whether they signaled relief or loss. Maybe both. He hadn't realized that joy and mourning could so cleverly intertwine.

But crying in the woods wasn't going to do him any good. He rose up on his knees—somewhat awkwardly, due to the weight of the backpack—and was about to stand when he heard a crash behind him, accompanied by a shout.

"Jesus Christ!"

Morli spun around.

Several paces away, Baxter was gaping back at him.

12

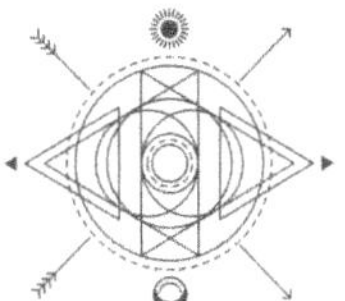

etting Morli go had been the hardest thing Baxter had ever done, but he knew he had no choice. It was the right course of action, dammit. But god, it hurt so much, as if he were that poor guy getting his heart torn out in *The Temple of Doom*. He did his best to stay strong, though. No use making Morli feel awful about leaving.

Baxter hadn't exactly been sad when Morli's attempts to use the feather had failed. Hey, they'd tried their best! Now they could go inside and bake something and snuggle up on the couch in front of a movie. Maybe Baxter would introduce him to *The Wizard of Oz*, a film that should resonate with Morli, even though Morli had done the equivalent of traveling from Oz to Kansas rather than the other way around.

Yeah, that was truly selfish.

So when Morli handed over the feather, Baxter took it, knowing deep in his heart that *this* was going to work. He was going to wish and Morli would disappear. Which is exactly what happened. There was a loud pop as Morli blinked away.

Before Baxter had time to react, the raven cawed and swooped right at him. He ducked—and felt himself yanked into an enclosed dark space, like a closet. *Like a coffin*, his brain had helpfully informed him. Otherwise unable to move, he opened his mouth to scream and was pushed hard from behind, lurching forward through something sticky and disturbingly like a thick spiderweb, and onto his knees.

"Jesus Christ!"

He opened his eyes to discover that he was in a forest. And Morli was a few yards away, mouth hanging wide.

Baxter rose almost to his feet, stumbled, got up again, and met Morli halfway. They clutched each other desperately.

"Are we— Is this— Did we—?" Baxter couldn't seem to string together a coherent sentence.

But Morli must have understood him anyway. He pulled back and gave Baxter a solemn nod. "My home. This is the Aksesh Forest."

"I AM SO SORRY," Morli said for what felt like the hundredth time., And for the hundredth time, Baxter shook his head. This wasn't Morli's fault at all, and he'd say so as soon as he could speak clearly. At the moment however, all he could do was sit on a large rock, holding his dizzy head to keep it from falling off.

Morli had dropped the backpack near Baxter's feet and was pacing back and forth, his shoes sending up little clouds of dried leaf pieces. None of the intact leaves looked familiar, nor did any of the trees, shrubs, or smaller plants. Baxter had been in extensive forests only a couple times in his life—there weren't any in or near Chicago, where he'd lived until this year—so he was no expert on the subject. But he was almost positive nothing in his world had purple flowers with tiny fangs in the middle of them.

Morli passed by him again. "I'm so sorry." He looked incredibly distressed, which wasn't fair. He'd wanted to go home and here he was; he should be relieved.

Guilt finally loosened Baxter's tongue. "Stop it. This isn't your fault."

"But I—"

"I did the magic, Morli. Me. I probably said something wrong and screwed things up."

"I didn't mean to steal you from your home."

Baxter grabbed Morli's hand. "I know you didn't. Now I'm here and we're going to have to deal. How about—" A thought struck him and he leapt to his feet. "Look!" He yanked the manila envelope from his back pocket.

Morli's eyes widened. "The third feather!"

"I forgot I had it. So see? It's fine. I can zap myself home." But he paused before reaching inside. "Unless...."

Oh, this was crazy. He was stupid. Except Morli was right there, and he was so extraordinary, and Baxter had been given only a small taste of him.

Baxter cleared his throat. "What if I don't go home right away?"

"What?"

"What if I stay with you? For a little bit. If you don't mind. I mean, if you want, I can leave and—"

"Stay!" Morli had broken into a wide grin. "Please. It's not... it's not Modesto, and we don't have televisions or Target or microwave ovens, but I'd like to show you a few things anyway. Show you my home." He appeared nervous, as if he honestly thought Baxter would refuse.

"I'd love to see your home." And spend more time with you, although Baxter didn't say that aloud. He didn't want to mislead Morli with any longer-term implication of connection. Baxter knew they couldn't have that, even though he desperately craved it.

Morli looked both excited and apprehensive. "What about your house? Your work?"

Baxter considered. He was a little ahead on his current project, and his boss wouldn't expect anything from him for a week. He had no pets to worry about. His garden might die due to lack of water, but the growing season was almost over anyway. His rent and utilities were paid for a couple more weeks at least. Some of the food in the fridge would spoil, but not much. He'd left the back door unlocked, so burglary was a possibility. But he had renter's insurance, and owned very little that was irreplaceable. A ransacked house would be worth a tour of another world—and more time with Morli.

He felt a tug in his gut at the realization that nobody would notice he was missing for several days. Nobody would care.

"It's fine," he said.

Morli held Baxter's hand and did a happy little dance, complete with a fancy twirl. He'd probably been taught all kinds of dances, since he was a prince. Baxter hadn't, unless you counted the middle-school square-dancing lessons in which he stomped on Jenny Chaudhary's foot so many times that he was finally banished to the corner of the gym, red-faced with shame.

When the celebration was over, Morli gave him a stern look. "You're not going to try to conquer the tower with me."

That hadn't occurred to Baxter, who wasn't thinking that far ahead. But now that Morli had said it.... "Why not? I can help." How, he wasn't sure, but he had to offer.

"You could get yourself killed. No. Absolutely not." For the first time, Morli sounded like a prince, his tone commanding.

"How far is the tower from here?"

Morli frowned. "I don't actually know. Aksesh Forest is huge, spanning several kingdoms, and I have no idea where within the forest we are. Um, or which way to go." He looked around uncertainly.

"I take it you don't have magical GPS."

"What's that?"

"It's... never mind. Do you know wilderness survival skills? How to find water, food, stuff like that?"

"No." Morli shook his head slowly. "Nobody expects a prince to get lost in the forest."

Baxter had never been a Boy Scout. He hadn't asked to join, and it had certainly never occurred to his parents to suggest it. They didn't sign him up for anything extracurricular when he was little. He'd come home from school, do his homework, and amuse himself with TV or books or the computer or the Lego sets Aunt Opal gave him for Christmas. None of those had taught him how to live in the wild. All he had was a vague idea that moss grew on the north side of trees, and he didn't know if that was accurate in his own world, let alone in Morli's.

"We won't starve right away," Morli pointed out. "We have muffins."

"Right. And a knife, some clothes, and a bottle of herbicide."

"And each other."

Yes. There was that. Baxter smiled at him.

Morli shouldered the pack and set off in what was, Baxter was fairly certain, a random direction. There was no trail, and for all Baxter could tell, they were walking in circles. One tree looked pretty much like the next. But at least the ground was level and the underbrush light enough for easy passage. Morli said his world didn't have poison oak, poison ivy, or venomous snakes. However, Baxter had the impression that there *were* some dangers that Morli chose not to mention. The purple flowers with tiny fangs came to mind.

Baxter felt thankful that he'd worn sneakers instead of flip-flops, but his feet grew tired anyway, and he tried to ignore his growing thirst. Morli didn't complain at all and, further, insisted on carrying the weighty backpack. Sometimes he'd point out a plant he was familiar with.

"Look!" he said, coming to a sudden stop and pointing. A tree several yards ahead of them was entwined by a snake-like vine with dinner plate–size leaves colored the mottled gray of a week-dead corpse.

"Choketree?" Baxter figured it was a safe guess.

"Yes. Don't walk too close. It can move fast."

"It eats *people*?"

"Not usually. But sometimes it doesn't know a person's not tasty until after it's wrapped itself around and smothered them. And by then it might as well eat them, for all the difference it makes to the person involved."

They gave it a wide berth. Baxter was slightly cheered to see it, however, because it was new to him, and that meant they weren't tromping in circles. They walked for what might have been a mile or might have been much more. It was hard to judge time through the tree canopy.

"A forest ranger would come in handy right about now," Baxter finally said.

"I don't know what that is, but all right. We're lucky, you know. With the weather, I mean. It won't get too cold tonight, not at this time of year."

Baxter thought about sleeping in the open in the middle of a forest—a forest containing killer plants—without even a tent for shelter. They had no flashlight and no matches to light a fire. Did that rubbing sticks thing really work? "I'm sorry I'm such a terrible outdoorsman."

Morli shrugged. "So am I. My main experience has been in the palace gardens. My first fling was with one of the gardeners, hidden behind a large and hideous statue of sleeping vedi. But that's about as much outdoor excitement as I've had."

Ignoring an irrational pang of jealousy, Baxter asked, "What's a vedi?"

"Ved, singular; vedi, plural. They look a bit like humans, but much bigger and hairier. They're covered in it from head to toe."

Huh. So Morli's world had its own version of Bigfoot. Interesting. "Why would someone make a statue of them?"

"This one is a memorial. They're good to have around the home. They protect families and help out with chores. They're very rare, though. I've only met one real one."

That was too bad. A ved might have been helpful in conquering the tower. Baxter was just ready to mention that when something shook the branches above them. He and Morli instinctively ducked as something hurtled toward them... and landed on a nearby low branch. It was a raven. *Their* raven, Baxter assumed.

Apparently so did Morli, who looked as cheerful as if greeting an old friend. "Hello! I was wondering where you were. Look who came back with me!"

The raven eyed Baxter and gave a noncommittal croak. "Uh, hi," said Baxter, who wasn't used to talking to birds.

Morli shrugged out of the backpack, dug around in it for a moment, and pulled out the Ziplock with the muffins. "We're willing to share. Could you help us find some water? And the best way out of here?"

The raven seemed to think about this for a few moments, maybe because muffins weren't as tasty as eyes. If she waited long enough, Baxter thought, he and Morli would probably drop dead and she could have her treats. But then she gave an affirmative-sounding caw. She took off, flying very low, her wing flaps surprisingly loud. With a triumphant grin, Morli quickly stuffed the muffins back in the bag, and he and Baxter hurried after her.

She led them at a fast pace and was probably annoyed with their slow human legs. But she didn't leave, and after a little while she brought them to a shallow but swift-running stream. She landed on a stone in the middle, looking pleased with herself. Morli and Baxter drank their fill; nothing had ever tasted as good. After splitting a muffin with the raven, the three continued on their way.

The sky was beginning to darken when they heard a commotion ahead. It sounded like lots of ravens squabbling with one another. And sure enough, when their little party reached the top of a slight rise, an entire flock of black birds occupied the space below them. In the center of the birds lay a purplish-brown lump the size of an SUV.

"What is *that*?" Baxter asked. It looked sort of like an oversized catfish, although that seemed unlikely in the middle of a forest.

"Basilisk. Dead, poor thing."

"Poor thing? Don't basilisks kill just by looking at you?"

Morli tsked at him. "That's a gross exaggeration and

pretty mean. Yes, they're so ugly they can't even stand to look at one another. That's why there aren't very many basilisks. But their looks aren't fatal."

"Are they dangerous at all, then?"

"This one's not."

Baxter rolled his eyes. "When they're alive, I mean. Are they dangerous?"

"No. They're very shy, I suppose because nobody wants to see one. My brother Algar caught a small one once and stuck it in my wardrobe to frighten me. Which it did, but I think it was twice as scared."

"What did you do?" asked Baxter, thinking that Algar sounded like a real piece of work.

"Wrapped it in a blanket and carried it out to the edge of the gardens, where the royal woods begin. I let it go." He gave a wicked smile. "But it had shit in my wardrobe, and I took that and hid it under Algar's mattress. He spent days trying to find the source of the stink."

Baxter couldn't help it; he tugged Morli in for a kiss.

"What was that for?" Morli's deep green eyes gazed up at him.

"I like you."

"I like you too."

While they were talking, their raven had flown down to join the others. She kept trying to land on the dead basilisk, but the other birds chased her away. They were pecking at the carcass, Baxter saw now, but aside from the empty eye sockets—which he didn't really want to look at—the ravens weren't having any luck turning the basilisk into dinner.

"That thing has a tough hide, huh?"

Morli nodded. "Scales. The one in my wardrobe felt as if it were wearing armor."

"What do you suppose killed this one?"

"No idea. It's pretty enormous, so maybe just old age." Morli sounded sad. "Poor thing, dying alone."

Baxter, mindful that Morli had also died alone, gave him a fierce hug.

The birds continued to quarrel, chasing away Morli's raven whenever she tried to come close. She was bigger and glossier than they were, which made it easy to spot her, but she couldn't take on a whole flock. Baxter was going to suggest that they move on and hope she came with, but Morli stomped down into the clearing, making all the other birds scatter to nearby branches.

"There's no point in all this fighting," he announced loudly. "You can't get past the scales anyway. Besides, there's more than enough for all of you to eat your fill." Again he rummaged in the backpack, this time producing the knife. "I'll tell you what. I'll try to open the carcass for you as long as you share with my friend. She's traveled a long way today and she's hungry."

The flock seemed to confer about this, clacking and croaking at one another. Baxter wondered whether they had any formal decision-making process. Maybe even leadership or government of some kind. Or maybe they operated as a committee, which meant the lot of them could be stuck here all day. Meanwhile, their raven dropped down and landed on Morli's shoulder. Baxter was slightly nervous about Morli's eyes, but the raven simply perched there looking regal and, he thought, a little smug.

The flock must have finally reached a decision. A few of them called, and Morli's raven flapped over to the basilisk and landed on its bumpy head. She looked at him expectantly.

"Good decision," Morli said with a smile.

He had to hack quite hard to make a long, deep incision

in the basilisk's side. Some slimy green intestines-looking stuff slithered out, making Baxter grateful his own stomach was mostly empty. "You eat pigs and cows," he reminded himself quietly. The ravens seemed delighted, hopping around in what seemed to be their own form of celebration.

Morli stepped away from the body, and while the birds swarmed forward to feast, he carefully wiped the knife clean with some soft leaves.

"I think we'll be here a while," he said when he rejoined Baxter. "Do you mind?"

"Not as long as I'm here with you."

They sat atop the rise, shoulder to shoulder, watching the birds. It was, Baxter thought, like the world's strangest date, and yet he felt more content than he'd ever been with an app hookup or barroom chat. It was gross but interesting to watch the ravens tear apart the basilisk—a live-action nature show without the commercials or tedious narration. And the human company was even better. Morli, close enough to touch, when Baxter had thought he'd lose him forever.

"I can't think of anyone I'd rather be lost in an alien forest with," Baxter said.

"Ditto. Although it's not alien to me."

They leaned against each other, silent for a long time. There weren't many insects, Baxter noticed. Flies buzzed around the carcass, along with some things that resembled large dragonflies, and he saw a few beetles trundling about. But no ants and no mosquitoes. No squirrels or other small creatures, either, and no birds except the ravens. "Are all your forests this empty?"

"No. People say Aksesh is cursed. Or maybe haunted. It depends who's telling the story."

Baxter glanced around warily, half expecting ghosts to leap out at them. "You don't seem worried."

"There's not really much I can do about it, is there? We'll deal with problems if they pop up." Morli sounded not exactly blasé, mostly just practical. And he was right—it was hard to plan for disasters when you had no idea what they might be and when your tools for addressing them were severely limited. It was a good attitude, albeit one that had already gotten Morli killed.

"You're good in a pinch," Baxter said thoughtfully.

"I'm what?"

"When stuff happens to you—bad stuff, even—you don't freak out and you don't complain. You landed in a new and unfamiliar world in a totally different body, and you pretty much took it in stride. I wouldn't have. I've been whining all day, actually, and I got to keep my original body. You're a strong man."

Morli was giving him a very strange look. "Strong? Do you really think that?"

"I know that."

"Oh." Morli ducked his head as if to hide his blush. "Nobody's ever called me that before."

"Then nobody's been paying enough attention."

Morli bumped his shoulder hard against Baxter's.

After another long silence, Baxter said, "Those ravens are really hungry."

"They probably don't get such a big feast very often. I bet within a few days there will be nothing left but scales and bones."

Baxter could imagine that. He was wondering how any of the ravens would fly, given the amount they were eating, and he hoped their raven wouldn't stick around too long. He wasn't especially eager to try raw basilisk, but the only food left in the backpack were three muffins.

"It's funny," Morli said, eyes trained on the flock.

He didn't say what was funny, but he tilted his head this way and that as if trying to understand something. "Ravens aren't very big and basilisks are. This one was, anyway."

"True."

"But in the end there'll be no more basilisk and a lot of fat ravens."

"Power in numbers, I guess."

Morli whirled to face him, smile wide and eyes shining. "Yes! That's it exactly!"

"That's what?"

"The solution!" Morli gave him a friendly thump to the chest. "All those people tried to rescue the princess, and every one of them died. Me included. Why?"

This felt like a pop quiz in school. "Because there's an enchanted bramble?"

"Yes, but in the end it's just a magicked plant. Some of those skeletons hanging with mine once belonged to great warriors. The most skilled swordsmen. But the plant won. Why?"

Baxter shrugged; Morli thunked him again. "Because we all tried to do it by ourselves! Imagine if one raven decided to strip that basilisk carcass all alone. It would never manage."

"Especially if you didn't slice it open first."

"Yes! Exactly!" This time Morli slapped his own thigh for emphasis. "And what about Frodo? He wouldn't have succeeded without help from Samwise and Merry and Pippin, and Gandalf, and the elves, and.... Well, you get my meaning."

Baxter didn't, at least not at first. He had to chew on it for a while before comprehension blinked on, like a neon sign. "Power in numbers. So you think the way to rescue the princess is to do it with a group."

"Yes! Nobody's tried it before, I suspect because they wanted the glory and the reward all to themselves. And the princess," he added with a sour expression. "All the stories mention only the great hero, not the people who helped the hero. So nobody thinks of that part."

"That makes sense."

Morli nodded decisively. "I'll gather a team and we'll beat the bramble together."

Baxter had some reservations. Not about the concept itself—the idea was good. But it might be hard to find people willing to risk life and limb for nothing but shared fame and a reward split multiple times. No use telling Morli, however, especially when he looked so pleased with himself.

"So now you know our first step when we get out of the forest," Baxter said.

Morli looked determined. "We recruit."

13

By the time the raven ate her fill, night had almost fallen. She didn't seem too keen on flying between trees in the dark, and Baxter and Morli kept tripping over roots and stones in the path. Besides, it was impossible to follow a black bird in an unlit forest. She found a nearby stream—or maybe just a different stretch of the one they'd seen before—and the three of them drank. Baxter and Morli each ate a muffin, and they all bedded down for the night. In the raven's case, that meant a nearby tree branch, where she arranged herself with some quiet croaks and feather ruffles.

Baxter and Morli found the softest spot of ground they could, tossed away some rocks, and used the backpack and some of Morli's spare clothing as pillows. Although the temperature was comfortable, they pressed close together, with Morli as the little spoon since Baxter was bigger and taller. Baxter tucked his nose near Morli's nape, the sweet yeasty smell of him a great comfort.

Yet despite that comfort, Baxter had a worry. "Will

anything eat us while we sleep?" He didn't even know what the potential predators might be. Bears? Wolves? Orcs?

"I hope not."

"But what if—"

"Sleep, Baxter." Morli pressed back against him, the roundness of his ass fitting perfectly into the cradle of Baxter's hips. "More adventures tomorrow."

Baxter sighed, yawned, and clutched him a little tighter.

IN THE MORNING they washed in the stream, and Baxter had to put on the same dirty, smelly clothing from the day before because Morli's didn't fit him. While they split the last muffin, the raven disappeared, probably to grab some breakfast from the basilisk. At least one of them would eat well.

Baxter tried very hard not to be grouchy. Nothing had gobbled them during the night, they had a guide, and Morli was at his side. All very good things. But he was sore from sleeping on the ground, and half a muffin wasn't much of a breakfast.

They followed the raven all the way through the morning and, Baxter suspected, most of the afternoon before the trees began to thin. Soon they were out of the forest entirely, walking across a meadow under a clear blue sky. Little flowers—yellow and pink and purple—dotted the grass, and a slight breeze kept the air from being too warm. It would have made for a lovely stroll if they weren't exhausted, starving, and lost. "Quests are a lot easier in video games," Baxter pointed out. "Plus if you die, you can start again."

"I did that."

"How do you feel about that?" They hadn't truly discussed the subject, mostly because Morli didn't seem interested and the topic made Baxter uneasy.

"Well, I wasn't happy about it at the time. It hurt. But now I'm used to this body, I suppose. Unless I look in a mirror and am reminded of how strange I look."

"You don't look strange."

Morli gave him a skeptical glance. "My hair? My eyes?"

"Not strange: unusual. I like the way you look."

That earned Baxter a sunny smile. Then Morli's expression turned serious. "Even if we're in Udrodia, nobody will recognize me. Which isn't really a problem. But I'm going to have to explain the way I look."

"If your goal is to recruit people, you probably don't want to mention that you died during your last stab at the tower."

"Good point. But I have to tell them something." Morli ran his fingers through his thick green locks. "I've never been a good liar. And even if I were, I'd be uncomfortable lying to them."

"You don't have to. But you don't have to tell the bald truth either. You can... pick and choose."

"Hmm. So what would I say about my hair and eyes?"

That was easy. "You were subject to an enchantment, but it hasn't diminished your abilities. Which is true, right?"

Morli shrugged. "Strictly speaking."

"That's all you tell them. Then you move on."

Although Morli looked doubtful, he complied. "All right."

Just when Baxter was wondering if the meadow stretched on forever, they came to a narrow dirt road rutted with wheel tracks. The raven turned left and flapped along the road for a few yards, then soared high and away without so much as a goodbye croak. Heading back to the basilisk, maybe, or perhaps she was just sick of their company. In any case, she'd led them out of the forest, for which Baxter was grateful.

The landscape was mostly flat now, with a few gentle rises here and there. The meadow on either side of the road eventually gave way to farmland, but it appeared as if the crops had been recently harvested.

"Are we going to stop there?" Baxter pointed toward a small stone house with a clay tile roof.

"No. There'll be a village soon, and that means an inn. We'll go there."

"We don't have any money." Baxter had been transported here without his wallet, and in any case, he was certain greenbacks, an ATM card, and a Visa wouldn't do them much good.

"I know." As usual, Morli was unperturbed.

They eventually came to a scattering of buildings that Baxter supposed counted as a village. Just a few dozen houses, all of them slightly resembling something from Middle Earth, and, at a crossroads, a little square with a well in the center, surrounded by two-story structures that were probably commercial buildings of some kind. There weren't many people around, but the few that they passed froze and stared, open-mouthed. Two small dog-like creatures with orange fur and weird yellow eyes chased after them, squawking, but didn't attack. Morli, looking regal with his chin held high, ignored them all.

He marched over to a bench near the well, where two old women and an equally ancient man sat knitting. Well, they had been knitting; now they just gaped. "Pardon me." Morli executed a perfect bow. "We're travelers from afar and we've lost our way. Can you tell me the name of this town?"

Town was pushing it, Baxter thought, but maybe Morli was trying to flatter the villagers. The three of them exchanged looks before the woman with wispy white hair spoke. "You're an odd-looking one."

"An enchantment, madam."

She sniffed. Maybe she didn't approve of enchantments, an opinion Baxter could empathize with. "And your clothes?" She had one tooth, large and surprisingly sharp, like a fang of the vampire at Marden's Magic Emporium.

"Standard where we come from, madam."

She sniffed at that too, then poked a knitting needle in Morli's direction. "This here is Stothwallow."

Morli looked relieved. "Ah, wonderful. Um, have you any recent news of the royal family?"

The trio broke into wheezy laughter. "The royal family?" said the man. "We don't have any need for that frippery around here. I doubt you do either." He resumed his work on an intricately patterned and colorful sock. Baxter hadn't yet been brave enough to try double-pointed needles, and he felt awed that anyone could work with so many needles and so many little balls of variously colored yarn all at once.

"Of course not. I was just curious. Thank you." Morli bowed again and headed toward the largest building on the square. He jerked his head for Baxter to follow. "We're in Udrodia," he said very quietly. "My kingdom."

"Is that good?"

"Could be. You're very big and look intimidating. That's good. But let me do the talking in here, all right?"

Baxter squared his shoulders, oddly pleased to be called

scary. He'd be perfectly happy if he didn't have to say a word to anyone; he was awkward enough with people in his own world.

When they entered, Baxter realized it was a tavern. An enormous fireplace stood against the far wall, containing nothing but ashes at the moment. A long bar of scarred wood ran the length of the space, and wooden tables of various sizes were scattered between upright support beams. Sawdust covered the floor. A dozen lanterns hung from the rafters, providing dim light, and everything smelled of sweat, old beer, and smoke. And cooking meat. Baxter's stomach growled.

Aside from a pair of stout middle-aged women behind the bar, there were only five other people in the tavern, none of them young. They goggled as brazenly as the knitters outside. Baxter hung back near the door, but Morli marched confidently to the bar. "Hello," he said sunnily.

The women looked highly skeptical, but they nodded. "'Lo," said the shorter one.

"My friend and I have traveled a very long way, and we're in need of meals and a night's lodging."

The same woman frowned. "We're the landladies here. We have food and a bed for a price."

"Well, that's where we have a small problem. We haven't any money at all, or any goods of value. We've been subject to a series of spells, you see, which have put us in an awkward position."

"We're not a charity."

"Of course not, madam. I'd like to offer you nonmonetary compensation."

The women snorted in unison. "Neither of us is interested in bedding men."

Baxter almost choked, but Morli's smile didn't dim one

bit. "That wasn't the compensation I had in mind, although I'm flattered you thought so. What we have to give you are fantastic tales of adventures in exotic lands. Tales nobody in Stothwallow has ever heard before."

Morli was incredibly charming; Baxter didn't see how anyone could refuse him. As the women stared at each other in silent conversation, the customers chimed in. "Say yes," urged a skinny old man. "It's not like you're overrun with guests."

A woman wearing a red scarf said, "Yeah, say yes. C'mon. Even if their stories are bad, some of us won't mind looking at 'em."

Grinning, Morli bowed deeply to the room at large.

"And you sweep up tonight," said the short landlady. "Help with the dishes."

"It would be our pleasure."

That settled, Morli led Baxter to a table near the fireplace. The chairs weren't very comfortable, but it was nice to sit. Nicer still when the taller landlady brought them large mugs of hard cider and bowls of some kind of stew. Thinking of the basilisk, Baxter didn't ask what the meat was. The food was tasty and filling, in any case, although Morli muttered under his breath about the quality of the bread.

The other customers didn't engage Morli and Baxter in conversation, but they continued to gawk and to eavesdrop shamelessly. Morli and Baxter remained mostly silent, which gave Baxter a good opportunity to observe how much more confident his companion was here than in Modesto. Baxter found an assured Morli very sexy indeed.

After the meal was over, the tall landlady took them up a set of creaking stairs and down a hall to the end room. It was sparsely furnished with a lumpy-looking bed, a wooden washstand, and a low bench. A couple of rag rugs adorned the floor, providing the only real color. There was a small fireplace with whitewashed brick, but it was unlit.

"I'm sure we'll be very comfortable here, madam. We'll take some time to rest and wash up if that's all right."

The woman made a noise that might have been assent before she left, shutting the door firmly.

Morli dumped the backpack onto the floor, sat on the bench, and removed his shoes. "Oh, that feels good!"

"They're really going to let us stay here just for telling some stories?"

"Of course. It's not like Modesto, Baxter. Nothing much happens in a village like this, and they don't have television or the internet. When a bard visits, that's a big draw. I'll bet most of the village squeezes in here tonight, and our hosts will have a very profitable night."

That made sense, but Baxter was stuck on one specific word. "Bard? Oh God, we don't have to sing, do we?" Sometimes he had nightmares about being forced to sing in public.

Morli chuckled. "No. Talking will be fine."

Well, that was a relief. Baxter sat next to him and pulled off his shoes and socks. Morli was right—bare feet felt wonderful. "Are you going to tell them about the tower?"

"No. Everyone in Udrodia knows about Princess Osenne already, and as you pointed out, it would be unwise for me to tell them what happened to me."

"What will you tell them, then?" Now that his socks were off, Baxter became acutely aware that they reeked. For that matter, so did he. He'd spent two days tromping through the forest in the same clothes. His teeth felt scummy too. God, what he would give for his bathroom back home. Which raised another unpleasant thought. He peeked under the bed, and... yep. Chamber pot. Great.

Apparently unaware of Baxter's hygiene distress, Morli rubbed his hands together. "I'm going to tell them about Frodo. They'll love that. And you...." He tapped his chin thoughtfully. "Star Wars, I think."

"You want me to tell these people about Luke Skywalker and Darth Vader?"

"They've never heard anything like it. They'll be entranced."

Baxter thought about speaking in front of a crowd and swallowed hard. "I'm not sure...."

Morli patted his knee. "It's all right if you don't want to. I simply thought they'd like it more if both of us spoke. You can be strong and silent if you'd rather."

Baxter *would* rather. Even the idea of public speaking made him feel slightly ill. What if he said something stupid and everyone laughed at him? What if he mangled the saga, or what if he got it right and everyone still hated it? What if....

Wait. Morli had faced an enchanted bramble even though he didn't want to, and he'd died for it. Baxter wouldn't die even if everyone in Stothwallow jeered at him. Probably. And he had made few if any significant contributions to their journey. The least he could do was sing for his supper, so to speak.

"I'll try."

Morli patted him again. "Good! It will be fun."

Although Baxter doubted that very much, he attempted a smile. Then he cast a look at his discarded socks. "I don't suppose there's a laundromat nearby."

"Take off your clothes," Morli ordered imperiously, hopping to his feet.

"But—"

"I'll do it for you." Now he waggled his eyebrows.

But Baxter wasn't feeling at all amorous, not when his own stink was heavy in his nose. He skimmed out of his clothing quickly—setting aside the envelope with the remaining feather—and Morli gathered up all of their soiled clothes. Wearing nothing but a longish T-shirt and boxer briefs, Morli left the room. That left Baxter naked and alone, with nothing much to do except gaze out of the window and onto a little courtyard below. Chickens scratched in the dirt, an extremely large cat dozed on a doorstep beside one of the dog things, and sheets flapped gently on drying lines. He thought that the little wooden building was probably an outhouse, but he couldn't identify the weedy little flowers growing here and there.

After about thirty minutes, Morli returned with a pile of fabric in his arms. "Borrowed these. Ours will be clean and dry by morning."

"How did you talk them into doing our laundry?"

"I showed them how to make muffins. No zucchini here, but we put in some grated heartroot instead, which should be tasty. And no muffin tins. We used clean flowerpots instead." He smiled proudly.

"That's smart."

"Do you want to rest a bit? I do."

As soon as Morli said it, Baxter remembered how exhausted he was. He hadn't slept well in the forest, and now the big meal felt heavy in his stomach, as if he were a snake who'd swallowed an elephant. "A nap would be great, but let's wash up first."

He followed Morli's lead, dipping a rough cloth in the washbowl and scrubbing away with a bit of soap that smelled like olive oil. They even cleaned their feet. Then, naked, they climbed into the bed, which turned out to be a little narrow for two men. The sheets were coarse, but they felt clean and smelled pleasant, a little like the meadow they'd walked through that morning. Baxter spooned with Morli, took a moment to savor the feeling of Morli's ass against his groin, and promptly fell asleep.

14

Morli's version of *The Lord of the Rings* proved incredibly popular. As he'd predicted, the inn was filled to capacity, with men and women and even some children perched on chairs, sitting on the floor, or leaning against the walls. The landladies beamed as they carried tankards and collected coins. And everyone in Stothwallow hung on Morli's every word. He had to explain a few things to them and change a few elements to fit their understanding, but overall Tolkien's world made an excellent transition to theirs. Morli drank three tankards of cider while he spoke, mostly to keep his throat wet, probably, and by the third he'd grown extra animated and was acting out all of the voices with great enthusiasm.

It was great fun to watch him.

When Morli finished, everyone clapped and cheered so wildly that Baxter was nearly deafened. "More! More! More!" they shouted.

"I don't know," Morli said. "It's quite late."

"We'll take up a collection!" shouted a young woman in the middle of the room. Her neighbors agreed immediately, one of them taking off a hat and everyone throwing in a coin or two.

Morli looked at Baxter, who shrugged. Then he turned back to the crowd. "Just give us a few minutes, please." He grabbed Baxter's wrist and dragged him out a back door and into the courtyard. The silence was wonderful.

The little shed was, indeed, an outhouse. They each took a turn using it and then washed up a bit at a nearby pump.

"It would be nice to have a little money," Morli said. "But I can tell them another story if you don't want to."

That was a tempting offer indeed. Baxter gave Morli's cheek a light caress. "I guess I can try. Please interrupt me if I'm awful."

"You won't be, but all right. Look, pretend I haven't seen the movie and tell the story to *me*. Ignore everyone else."

Baxter wasn't sure how he was supposed to ignore a hundred or so people, most of whom were now at least a bit tipsy. But for Morli's sake, he'd try. He would be brave.

He almost changed his mind when they entered the inn, and then again when he stood in front of the big fireplace, gazing out at the sea of faces. Morli performed an introduction. "My friend Baxter comes from very, very far away. A kingdom so distant you've never even heard of it. Modesto! And tonight he'd like to share a story from his land. Can you be a little patient with a stranger from afar?"

Everyone whistled and hooted and clapped, and the hat made a second round. Morli politely managed to dislodge a man from a chair in the front row. Baxter closed his eyes, counted backward from twenty, and tried not to puke. When he opened them again, there was Morli with his green hair and bright green eyes, watching him with full confidence.

"Well," Baxter began. He cleared his throat and started

again. "Well. This happened a long time ago in a gal— in a kingdom far, far away."

The people of Stothwallow loved the story. They hissed at Darth Vader, cheered for Leia, and swooned over Han Solo. Baxter modified some of the details to keep the tale land-based, and he substituted mythological creatures—that may not have been so mythological in this place—for aliens and robots. But the plot and characters remained essentially true to the originals, and the locals ate it up. So much so, in fact, that they pleaded with him when he came to the end of Episode IV, and—with the rejuvenating help of cider, a big chunk of grilled meat, and Morli's improvised muffins—Baxter continued all the way through episodes V and VI as well.

There were genuine tears when Anakin died in Luke's arms, applause when the Death Star exploded, and a huge round of celebration when Han and Leia kissed. By then Baxter's voice was hoarse and his limbs felt heavy. Their landladies beamed as if they'd won the lottery. And Morli had never once taken his eyes off Baxter.

The landladies had to shoo away the crowd. They excused Morli and Baxter from their cleanup duties, which was good because Baxter wasn't sure he had the strength. He barely made it to the outhouse and up the stairs to their room. But then he got to skim off his borrowed clothing—a scratchy tunic and too-short leggings—and get into bed with Morli.

And then somehow, maybe by magic, Baxter found a bit more energy after all. As they spooned, they rocked gently together, Baxter's dick nestled perfectly in the cleft of Morli's ass and Morli's hard, hot dick in Baxter's palm. Baxter inhaled Morli's scent and licked his skin. Morli whimpered and chanted Baxter's name. Their climaxes were long and slow and sweet.

This is perfection, Baxter thought.

As PROMISED, their clothing was clean and dry by morning. The landladies fed them a generous breakfast of fried fish and fruit and something that resembled, but wasn't, oatmeal. "Would you like to stay another night?" the short woman asked hopefully. "Or two?"

"That's very generous of you, madam, but we have to be on our way. We have a quest to fulfill. In fact, I'd like to discuss this with the village."

Baxter had almost forgotten that part. Perhaps because he was having such an interesting adventure even without thorny vines, towers, or comatose princesses. He sighed.

It was a beautiful morning, the sky an unmarred blue, the temperature warm but not too warm, the air smelling of cut grass. Morli stood by the well in the center of the little square, the backpack at his feet. It was heavier now due to the considerable number of coins they'd collected, and he'd told Baxter that when they found a good smith, he'd buy two swords. He'd promised sturdy boots too. But for now he wore his Target sneakers, jeans, and pale blue T-shirt. His hair shined gloriously in the sun.

"Thank you for your company and generosity last night," he said to the assembled villagers. "Baxter and I so enjoyed your hospitality."

"Tell us more about Frodo!" someone yelled.

Morli smiled. "Not now, sadly. We can't stay. But I would like to ask for your help."

A slight ripple of uneasiness passed through the crowd.

Baxter, standing silent at Morli's side, watched people exchange glances and shift their feet. A few people at the back of the crowd slipped away.

But Morli plowed on. "I'm sure you've all heard about Princess Osenne, who's held in enchanted captivity in a tower in Vraelum. Many brave heroes have tried to rescue her, to no avail. But Baxter and I have a plan! We'd like you to join us in attacking the brambles as a team. We can all split the reward, and everyone will have a tale to pass down to their grandchildren. Will you come?"

Crickets. Well, not actual crickets, which might not have existed here, but metaphorical ones: a complete and stone-faced silence. More people left, this time without stealth.

"It's a lot of money, even shared," Morli said loudly.

A young woman near the front scoffed. "Money won't do you no good when you're dead."

Morli could have pointed out that he was appreciating everyone's coins just fine despite being dead, thanks very much, but he didn't. Instead he said, "But you probably won't die. Not with all of us chipping in."

The woman made a sour face and walked off. In ones and twos, so did everyone else. One older man with a friendly face paused. "You're welcome to stay here a while if you like. But don't go after that princess. It's a fool's errand."

"I have to," Morli said sadly.

"Then you're a fool." The man left too.

The square felt very empty, and Baxter ventured a question. "What do we do now?"

Morli heaved a mighty sigh and shouldered the heavy pack. "We try at the next village."

THEY PASSED through a few tiny hamlets that day. People stared but didn't speak to them, not even the pinch-faced man who sold them a lunch of fruit-studded bread and pickled vegetables. "Not bad bread," Morli said as they walked. He'd been quiet all morning, his shoulders sagging, but he'd refused to let Baxter take a turn carrying the pack.

Shortly before nightfall they came to a village that was several times larger than Stothwallow. This one boasted several inns, and Morli chose the biggest. They paid for their room and board—no stories this time—and bedded down in a room that smelled faintly of cooking grease. They didn't make love. In the morning, Morli again tried his recruitment speech, but the locals either ignored him or laughed. He and Baxter moved on.

This became their routine for the next few days, with Morli growing more reserved after each failed effort. He didn't convince a single person to join them, but he did collect jeers and catcalls. More than once, Baxter had to stop himself from punching a heckler who was making Morli feel bad.

A few times Morli told Baxter to return home, but his statements lacked conviction and he looked relieved when Baxter refused. At first Baxter had worried a little about his house and job, but the longer he spent with Morli, the less important everything in Modesto seemed.

"I thought it was such a good plan." Morli sighed as they lay in a narrow bed under a low roof.

Baxter had been hearing things scurrying in the corners since they'd doused the light, and he didn't want to know what those things might be. He stroked Morli's hair. "It is a good idea. These people are too blind to see it."

"They're my people, technically speaking. My father can give such rousing, inspirational speeches that everyone cheers about having their taxes raised. He doesn't say much in private, but give him an audience and he can do anything. I obviously didn't inherit that skill."

"You have lots of other skills. At least you're brave enough to try. I can barely speak in front of strangers."

Morli sighed again and shortly fell asleep.

The next day they came to the largest village yet. This one was a small city, really, with several squares and a lot of activity. It must have been a market day, because one of the squares was crammed with stalls selling food, household goods, and personal items. There was even entertainment in the form of a wheezy band and a small troupe of acrobats. "Watch for pickpockets," Morli warned.

Horrified at the implications, Baxter moved the envelope with the remaining feather to his front jeans pocket. He wished he had one of those security pouches for tourists, the kind like Rick Steves sold, and he wondered if anyone in this world had invented something similar.

Morli bought them some grilled mystery meat on sticks and a basket of sweet purple berries that stained their fingers. Then he paused in front of a merchant selling footwear and spent a long time closely inspecting the selection of boots. Eventually satisfied by their quality, he haggled with the merchant—a young woman with bright blonde hair—and ended up buying two pairs. Baxter's boots were shin-high and fashioned from reddish-brown leather, whereas Morli's reached his knees and had green embroidered flowers that matched his hair.

After that, they visited a booth stocked with gleaming knives and swords in a variety of sizes and shapes. Morli spent even longer there, picking up the swords and waving them around in a way that seemed to impress the two male vendors. At last he chose a particularly wicked-looking weapon, which apparently came with a plain leather scabbard and belt. Then he turned to Baxter. "Which one catches your eye?"

"Catch my eye is exactly what I'm likely to do with any of them. Or even more likely, catch some innocent bystander's." The most recent sword he'd handled had been a plastic lightsaber when he was nine, dressed as Obi-Wan Kenobi for Halloween.

"Hmm." Morli scrunched up his mouth in thought. "How about a dagger then?"

A dagger would be kind of cool, Baxter had to admit, and also probably less accidentally lethal. He picked one with a stylized raven on the handle; it seemed appropriate. When he hung the belt and sheath around his hips, he definitely felt more badass. Morli grinned, looking happier than he had in several days.

They bought some roasted nuts, sat on a stone bench at the edge of the square, and changed their footwear. It was pleasant just to stay put for a while and people-watch. The nuts looked unusual but tasted a little like macadamias.

"Are we spending the night here?" Baxter asked. It was only a little past noon, so he thought they might continue onward.

"Might as well, I guess. Not that I'll have any more luck here."

"You don't know that."

"Yes I do." Morli slumped.

Unsure of how to comfort him, Baxter gazed around. The nearest vendor was selling hair ribbons and other small adornments, and it was fun to watch people browse. The merchant, a grandmotherly type, would hold up a mirror so prospective buyers could admire themselves with the items, and she gushed at how the ribbons brought out the color in their eyes or how the lace cuffs made them resemble nobility. When a buyer settled on an item and they'd agreed on a price, the merchant would pause, look thoughtful, and muse, "You know what? I think you'd look even better if you added *this*." She'd hold up another item. "I can give it to you at a discount since you're such a good customer." It worked very well.

Baxter bumped shoulders with Morli. "That ribbon woman is really good at sales. If she were in my world, I bet she'd have catchy jingles or infomercials or something."

"Infomercials?"

"They're on TV. Someone pretends to be teaching you about something, but really they're pimping their product. It's an advertising technique. It used to be fairly effective, I think."

"Like Mr. Saucy?" Morli managed a hint of a smile.

"No infomercials for him. But they've been talking about an app—a game you can play on your phone. I don't know what kind of game might involve anthropomorphic barbecue sauce, but that wasn't my responsibility. I think they were also hoping for merch sales—Mr. Saucy kitchen towels, bottle openers, dog toys, T-shirts, whatever. Anything to make a buck." He lifted the basket of nutshells in a salute. "All hail the power of advertising."

And then it hit him, like an anvil dropping onto a cartoon character's head, and he let the basket slip in his excitement, scattering the empty shells on the cobblestones. "Advertising!"

Morli looked at him as if questioning his sanity. "What?"

Baxter wanted to kiss him. "I know how you can recruit people for your quest!"

"How?"

"Let's go somewhere quiet and I'll explain."

15

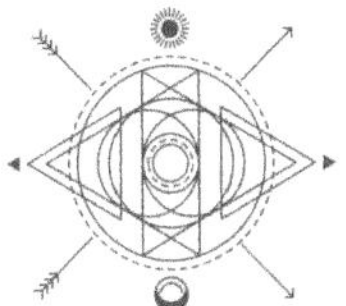

The *somewhere quiet* turned out to be a cramped room at an inn that had seen better days. They'd collected a lot of coins back in Stothwallow, but after paying for local clothing, boots, blades, and a week's worth of food and lodging, a bit of scrimping seemed in order.

Baxter didn't particularly care about the luxury of their surroundings. He was happy for time with Morli wherever they spent it. And now he had an idea.

"What's your plan?" Morli sat on the edge of the low bed, picking absently at the threadbare blanket. A glimmer of hope had appeared in his expression.

"Advertising." Baxter was on the room's only chair, a wobbly antique that held his weight uncertainly.

"Advertising?"

"Think about it—you're trying to persuade people to do something they don't especially want to do. Just like a company wants to persuade people to buy their stuff. And you can't just stand there and say, 'Buy my stuff. It's good.' Nobody will pay any attention."

Morli leaned forward, brow furrowed. "Like Mr. Saucy?"

"Right! You've been to the grocery store with me; you saw. There's at least a dozen brands of barbecue sauce for people to choose from, so how do you get them to pick yours? And let's assume they all taste pretty decent, so that's not a factor."

"Advertising!" Morli said, grinning.

Baxter stood, took two short strides to cross the room, and plopped down next to Morli. "Like I said, you can't just tell 'em to buy your sauce because it's good. You need more than that. So you give them an *image* that will appeal to them. You suggest that if they buy your sauce they'll feel like they're riding the range in Texas or grooving at a blues club in Kansas City. Or hanging out with snarky, cool pals like Mr. Saucy. They're not buying your sauce—they're buying the concepts that go with it."

Morli had stopped attacking the blanket and now rubbed under his nose instead. "Concepts. Like what?"

"Depends on the product. Could be adventure. Popularity. Sexiness—that's a big one. Health. Nostalgia. Eco-friendliness. Family. Luxury. Sophistication. Anything people want more of. You offer them more of that, and your product just sort of comes along for the ride."

"Isn't that dishonest?"

Oh. That. Baxter fell back on the mattress to stare at the ceiling beams. They were splintery and adorned with spiderwebs. "You can't outright lie. Where I come from, they have laws about that. So I can't tell people, 'Use my sauce and you'll gain thirty IQ points and inherit a million dollars.' But I *can* suggest. 'Use my sauce and you might feel really hip.' It's not entirely a lie, because when they buy the sauce they *will* feel hip."

These were ideas that Baxter had struggled with back

when he chose a career path. He'd decided that advertising for consumer goods wasn't a terrible thing—people were used to it, entertained by it even. He might have felt differently if asked to work on political campaigns, but luckily that had never happened.

After a moment, Morli fell back too. Baxter gazed at his face, only inches away. It would have been nice to run fingers through that soft green hair, but now wasn't the time.

"How do I use this to recruit people?"

"Begin by figuring out what people want."

"Not to go tromping for days and sleeping on the ground. Not to leave their homes and families just to rescue a princess from another kingdom." Morli sighed. "Not to die in a bramble."

Baxter took his hand, interlacing their fingers. "No. But let's consider the average young man or woman living in this city. Not the rich ones. The ones who work as brewers or tailors or... I don't know. Candlemakers." He still had only a vague idea of how people lived in Morli's world. "The ones who never leave the city and don't have a lot of variety in their lives. What do they want?"

"Well, money. Most everyone wants that. I told them about the reward, though, and it didn't work."

"Something more aspirational. Something more emotional."

Morli was quiet for several minutes, and Baxter waited. They were in no hurry. In fact, Baxter's own aspirations ran toward lying on a bed next to this man, so he was satisfied to wait forever.

"Excitement," Morli finally said. "Something outside their daily routine. Fellowship. A sense of accomplishing something important. A story they can tell their neighbors."

Baxter kissed Morli's knuckles. "There you go. And if

your quest succeeds—hell, even if it doesn't—won't they honestly get all those things?"

"As long as they don't die, yes."

"Then you just have to make sure they live."

After a few more minutes, Morli sat up. "I want to try this. Let's go."

"Are we leaving today?" Baxter hoped not. He wanted another night alone in a bed with Morli.

"No. In the morning I think."

"Then wait until then. If you give your speech now, they'll have time for second thoughts. That's another advertising principle—you want your customers to act fast. Supplies are limited! This offer expires soon! Operators are standing by!"

Morli may not have understood the references exactly, but he nodded. "This is all very strange for me. I've never given speeches before, and nobody's paid me much attention."

"Well, you're doing a damned good job of it."

"I'd never pictured myself doing much more than baking bread."

And since the pandemic had worsened, Baxter had never imagined more than living in his little house in Modesto, working on the computer, exercising, and taking up hobbies to get him through the solitude. Yet here he was.

"When I was little, I used to beg Great-aunt Opal to wave her wand or cast a spell to change my parents. To make them...." *To make them love me.* "To make them a better mom and dad." He'd never admitted this before. Never revealed to anyone how deep his hurt had been.

"I can understand that. I might have done the same if I'd known a sympathetic witch."

"Yeah, well Aunt Opal was sympathetic, but she said that

was too much magic for her to manage. She told me that you can't always control your situation, but you can control how you react to it." He hadn't always listened to that advice, but it was good advice nevertheless.

Morli looked down at him with a small smile that gradually brightened. "I know how I'd like to react right now. Maybe kill some time?" He waggled his eyebrows.

Baxter tugged him from his sitting position back down onto the bed.

"WELL," said the landlord. "I bet you two've worked up an appetite."

Baxter blushed hotly, suddenly aware of how vocal they'd been while killing time that afternoon. But Morli just gave a roguish smile. "And we need to gather our strength for later."

The landlord laughed and shook his gray-haired head. "Ah, youth! They say age brings wisdom, but I'd trade a lot of that for a little of a young man's stamina." He drew them each an oversize mug of cider and promised to have food ready soon.

The inn's dining area held only a half-dozen tables, all of them scarred by decades of use. Like their room, it was a little shabby, and it looked as if a broom hadn't reached the corners for a long time. It was comfortable, though, with a small fire despite the temperate evening and with the low murmur of conversation among the other customers. The landlord seemed to know everyone well, except Morli and Baxter. He moved across the floor in no particular hurry, clapping people's shoulders and briefly joining their conversations.

"That's a happy man," Morli observed.

Baxter agreed, feeling a little envious. He'd always wanted to be like Aunt Opal, cheery and content, but had never quite managed it. Except during his time with Morli.

"I wonder if being an innkeeper is a good profession," Baxter mused.

"I guess nearly anything is a good profession as long as you enjoy it. I had a brief fling with a stonemason once. He caught my attention because he was always humming and whistling, even when he was doing heavy work or the weather was vile. I asked him why and he told me there was nothing more satisfying than repairing or building someone's home. Making all the pieces fit, he said. Do you feel that way about your job?"

"Not really," Baxter admitted. "I like it, but I'm not passionate about it."

Morli nodded. "I'd be passionate about being a baker. If I had your Aunt Opal's magic wand, that's what I'd do. I'd make the finest bread in the kingdom." His eyes glittered at the thought.

"You could, you know. Let someone else deal with the princess."

"No. I have to try."

Baxter had known he'd say that but felt obligated to offer the alternative nonetheless. "What about after you rescue her?"

"I...." Morli looked blank, as if that question hadn't occurred to him. "After? I... I'm the prince." He didn't sound happy about that.

"But you don't have to be. Nobody's ever going to know it's you unless you tell them. This is your chance, Morli. Start a new life—the one you want instead of the one forced on you." Something about his own words echoed meaningfully in Baxter's head, but he didn't know why. He pushed the echo aside.

"I.... I suppose that's true."

"Something to think about, anyway."

Morli grabbed Baxter's hand across the table. "Yes. A good thought indeed."

The food was lackluster, but there was plenty of it and the company was pleasant. The landlord stopped by their table often to joke and banter. He told them about his husband, who'd died too young. "Wish I'd had him longer. But we fit several lifetimes worth of love into a few years."

A few years, Baxter thought. He'd give anything for that. He and Morli would have only a few weeks.

They had energy for a second round that night, with Morli howling Baxter's name loud enough to wake the entire city. Despite the hard narrow bed, they both slept deeply.

THE CROWD GATHERED ROUND them in the square, shifting restlessly. Baxter had already learned that it was easy to attract an audience, but harder to maintain one. "Are you ready?" he whispered to Morli.

"Yes." And Morli did look ready. He was handsome and confident, shining like a bright jewel among the drab earth tones that surrounded him. It was a mystery why nobody realized he was royalty, because he held himself like a prince. He leaned close to Baxter. "How about you?"

Baxter's stomach was doing gymnastics, but he smiled anyway. "Ready as I'll ever be." He and Morli had discussed strategy last night, and the one they'd chosen required Baxter to play a particular role. He didn't like that role, but he wanted to support Morli as fully as possible, and this was the best he could do.

Baxter took a step forward and stood with hands on hips. He wore clothing he'd purchased here: a pair of brown leggings somewhat looser than tights but still form-fitting, a cream-colored tunic with blue embroidery around the collar, and his new boots. His knife was at his hip. He'd grown a mustache and short beard since his arrival in this world, and thanks to the pandemic, his hair was longer than usual, falling to his shoulders. He felt as if he were cosplaying, but Morli told him he looked tough and rather dashing. "A bit of a rogue," Morli had said. "Like Han Solo."

Baxter stood straight-backed, knowing he towered over most of the locals, who tended to be on the short side. Thanks to his recent adventures, he'd lost much of his extra padding and unveiled solid muscles. He hoped he looked imposing—and nowhere near as terrified as he felt.

Ignoring his racing heart, Baxter spoke. He didn't quite yell, but he did project. "Ladies and gentlemen! My master has chosen *you* among all of Udrodia. Are you worthy?" His voice didn't even waver, and as expected, everyone's ears perked up. He knew his accent sounded a little exotic here, which was a good thing since Morli was about to sell excitement and novelty. He gave a deep bow to Morli—he'd practiced last night until Morli said it was perfect—and stepped back.

Morli lifted his chin and gazed out at the audience, as if assessing them. He and Baxter were dressed similarly, but the green embroidery on his collar matched that on his boots, and both emphasized his striking coloring. He held one hand loosely on his sword and stood with his legs wide, looking ready to leap into a duel at any moment. He was entirely, breathtakingly handsome and might as well have invented the word *regal*.

Baxter remembered the times Morli had sobbed in his arms, and he admired him all the more. Morli wasn't afraid to show his sorrow or his strength.

I love him.

The realization shook Baxter to the core, but he couldn't show it because now wasn't the time. His job was to look big and tough and scary, and dammit, he was going to do that if it killed him.

After a slight nod to acknowledge Baxter's introduction, Morli took a step forward. The crowd was silent, riveted. Even one of the meandering doglike creatures, which Morli called salawas, stopped scratching itself and cocked its head as if listening.

"I have an opportunity to offer. But I offer it only to those select few who are up to the challenge." As Baxter had instructed, Morli's voice didn't boom. In fact, those in the back might be straining a bit to hear it. That added to the mystique and made people feel as if they were privy to a secret. "I am looking for comrades to join me on the adventure of a lifetime. We will face risks, but we will be fierce, and smart, and we will overcome them. And when we triumph, our names will be remembered for generations!"

Overplaying it a bit, maybe. But Baxter figured that if you were, say, a tanner or a servant in a town where juggling was considered thrilling entertainment, this message might appeal. Especially if you'd grown up on stories of heroes conquering ogres and giants and the most interesting thing you'd done was sweep the little red roach-things out of the bedrooms before guests arrived.

"We will depart in one hour," Morli continued. "So if your ties to this place are too tight or you hesitate at discomfort, I'm afraid I'll have to refuse your service. We need people who can jump into action at a moment's notice."

Nobody wandered off. In fact, they leaned forward, eyes shining with excitement. When Baxter was in fifth grade, there was a boy named Phillip Cadwallader, a string-beany boy with untamable yellow hair. He sometimes sat with Baxter in the lunchroom, although they weren't close friends. In class, Phillip begged to sit in the front row, and he waved his hand wildly every time the teacher asked a question. Even when the teacher hadn't yet reached a question, Phillip would squirm and prepare himself like a runner on the starting block, as if he would absolutely *die* if he wasn't called on. Morli's audience resembled him now, a hundred Phillips who couldn't wait to be chosen.

But Morli was still speaking. "Our company will be victorious over an adversary that has defeated the weak and the foolish. We will rescue Princess Osenne and come home wealthy and swathed in glory."

"Princess Osenne?" shouted a woman in the middle of the crowd. "In the tower with the brambles?"

"The very same, madam."

"Prince Morli got himself killed trying to save her."

Morli didn't even flinch. Instead he bowed his head. "I have heard this sad news, and I mourn with you. But... was he a great warrior?"

The people looked at one another. Then a man spoke up. "I hear he made cakes."

"Baking is an admirable endeavor, sir. But does it prepare one for battle?"

"Well, no. I suppose not."

Morli nodded. "And royalty... they live quite pampered lives, I expect. Everybody fetching things for them all the time. They don't know about the benefits of hard work and persistence. Not like people who labor with their hands and their muscles and their brains, sir. I daresay a prince might be fine for choosing pastry or modeling the latest fashions, but when it comes to getting real things done, I'd take a working man or woman any day."

This was met with clapping and shouts of approval. Nobody else interrupted as Morli laid out his instructions. Interested parties were to gather their weapons and enough goods for five days of travel, then meet back at the square in forty-five minutes to see whether they passed muster.

Baxter stepped protectively in front of Morli and scowled. The crowd scattered.

He wanted to take Morli into his arms and tell him how wonderful he'd been, but too many people still watched, and Baxter was supposed to be his employee. His henchman. That made Baxter grin.

"Do you think any of them will return?" Morli whispered. His expression was blank, but Baxter clearly heard his anxiety.

"Yes."

Baxter was about ninety-five percent sure that was true.

16

They stood resolutely in the square, hoping they looked confident that recruits would arrive at any moment. The salawa strolled over to sniff at them, and when Morli rubbed its head, it wagged its forked tail. Then it curled up nearby and went to sleep.

After twenty tense minutes, two burly young men trotted up. Brothers, by the look of them, each smiling earnestly and carrying a pitchfork. They had horseshit on their boots and a manner that reminded Baxter of Jethro Bodine from *The Beverly Hillbillies*. "We're ready!" the beefier one announced. "We know all about workin' hard and stickin' to things." They were, Baxter thought, the most beautiful creatures he'd ever seen.

The woman who'd mentioned Prince Morli's death arrived next. She said she'd always wanted to meet a princess, and maybe this one might be worth marrying. Then came a man in a blacksmith's apron, a group of young men who looked like medieval frat bros, and a fortyish woman clutching an enormous cleaver. After that... a flood, until the square was nearly filled with people brandishing weapons, carrying packs, and raring to go.

Morli maintained his noble mien, but Baxter could tell he was beside himself with happiness. As Baxter watched, Morli passed through the throng, welcoming people with handshakes. He turned away a few people—underaged children and a couple of elderly folks who could barely totter across the square—but only after he had praised their bravery and begged them to keep the city safe in his absence. They went away only a little dissatisfied.

In the end, over sixty people joined them.

With Morli at the lead, they marched out of the square in a cheerful parade. Bystanders mostly stared, but several cheered them on, which made the recruits step higher. Soon they were on a road lined with fields and farmhouses. Morli had warned that they'd need to walk for over two full days to reach their destination, and Baxter had been concerned that people might lose their interest over that time.

Now his worries faded. Morli worked the crowd endlessly. He chatted with every individual at length, sharing jokes and asking about their life and their family. They ate it up, following at his heels like puppies and glowing under his attention. Somewhere along the line he discovered that one man was a professional bard, and after that, the bard led the group in occasional singalongs. Everyone was having a lovely time, even if all they were doing was marching through pretty, albeit repetitive, bucolic scenery.

Baxter kept mostly to himself, which suited both his nature and his role. Yet he didn't feel like an outsider, not when Morli always returned to his side.

Late that afternoon, when the sun threw long shadows and cows were returning to their barns, they came to a large crossroads. Morli didn't pause, but something in the set of his mouth caught Baxter's attention. "Is something wrong?" They were slightly ahead of the troop, and Baxter kept his voice low.

"If we turned left, we would have reached my home in several days. The capital."

"Do you want to go there?"

Morli shook his head. "Not now. Maybe not ever." Then he sighed. "It's a nice city, though. The Wornet River flows through it, crossed by the Seven Sisters bridges. You can sit at outdoor taverns along the upper banks and watch the little boats float by. At this time of year, the trees in the royal park are turning color. And there's a bakery on Goldwish Street that makes the most exquisite cornbreads. I've never been able to replicate them." He sounded wistful, and Baxter longed to hug him.

"You can go after the rescue is complete."

"And do what? Return to the palace and see if they'll believe who I am? I suppose I could convince them eventually, but...."

"Won't they be happy you're alive?"

Morli shrugged. "They're probably relieved to be rid of me."

"Morli!" Baxter exclaimed, shocked. His own parents hadn't really wanted him, but they certainly didn't wish him dead.

"We're strangers, Baxter. I was born to them and grew up with them, but we never really knew or understood one another."

"Morli—"

"I'm sorry. I didn't intend a bout of self-pity." He gave a weak smile. "I'll be all right."

"You will be, because you can make your own way in the

world. Look what you've accomplished. You managed an entire new world very well, and when you returned home, you landed right on your feet."

"Because I had you. I haven't done these things alone."

Baxter had been trying to ignore the tight band that constricted his heart every time he thought about leaving. But there it was, constricting him mercilessly. He tried to breathe through it. "I'm joining in with the rescue," he announced.

"No! It's dangerous. We discussed this. You'll go home before we attack the bramble."

"I will not. I'm a part of your army now."

Morli glanced back at the cheerful people trailing them. "It's not really an army. And Baxter, you have a whole life to live in Modesto."

A whole life. With nobody for company except Mr. Saucy and his dead Aunt Opal. With baked goods he had to make and eat by himself and a garden nobody enjoyed but him. With his mediocre job. With no plans or ambition for the future. With air he couldn't breathe and deadly viruses and so much existential angst he wanted to curl into a ball.

"I'm going to the tower," Baxter insisted. "And you can't stop me. You're not really my boss, and you're not my prince."

"What am I then?" Morli demanded.

The love of my life.

Baxter shrugged. "My leader, I guess. So lead on."

THEY SPENT the night in a newly tilled field, where the earth proved somewhat forgiving to tired bodies. The farming family had been more than a little surprised to see a horde arrive but, likely attracted by the novelty of the event, had offered their land for the night. They even joined the crew for prebedtime fireside storytelling. It was a convivial evening, and once again Baxter felt included, even though he spoke mostly to Morli.

When the time came, everybody spread out blankets to sleep on. Morli and Baxter kept a little distance between them, but not so much that they couldn't find each other's hands in the darkness. The ground was as comfortable as some of the lumpier inn beds. And above them, the sky spread generously, with two crescent moons and a show of stars so thick that Baxter felt he could reach up and run his fingers through them like jewels.

"I've never seen so many stars," he whispered to Morli.

"You could barely see the sun through your smoke."

"True. But even when the sky's clear back home, it's not like this. Light pollution, I guess. Anyway, this is beautiful."

Morli squeezed Baxter's hand. "One of the royal sorcerers claims she can tell people's futures by reading the stars. I don't believe her, though. She said I'll rise above the king and queen, and that's ridiculous. Even if I'd wanted the throne—which I didn't—three of my brothers have heirs of their own. I'm something like tenth in line for the crown."

"Maybe it's metaphorical. Like... you'll be above them ethically because you're a better person."

"Right." Morli snorted.

"Do you have constellations? Pictures you can make by connecting the star dots?" Back in his own world, Baxter could identify only the Big Dipper and Orion's Belt.

"Of course. Do you see that ring of stars over there?" Morli pointed.

Baxter didn't—there were just too many to discern actual shapes—but he said yes anyway.

"That's the wheel that fell off Zulraja's cart. She was a troll who bullied people into giving her their valuables, and then she'd take away the bounty in her cart. But a clever young woman named Estrid loosened a wheel, and it rolled away. Now Zulraja chases it through the sky—see? There she is—while Estrid laughs and returns everyone's goods to them over there."

Baxter laughed. "What happens when Zulraja finally catches it?"

"Oh, she'll stomp back to her wagon and be very angry. But by then Estrid and the others will be gone."

"What if Zulraja comes after her?"

Morli thought for a moment. "Imonar the Sorcerer will help. That's Imonar over there—a round person known for their kindness to those in need. They heal the sick, revive withered crops... that sort of thing. Imonar is also supposed to be an extremely skilled and generous lover. That cluster of stars over there are people hoping that Imonar will take them to bed."

"Mmm." Baxter felt pleasantly drowsy, like when Aunt Opal used to lull him to sleep with bedtime stories. "Nice to know not all sorcerers are assholes."

"Of course not! You're not, for instance."

"But I'm not a sorcerer."

For several minutes, Morli was quiet. Baxter thought he might have fallen asleep, but then Morli stirred and squeezed his hand again. "You are, you know. A sorcerer."

Baxter spluttered. "I am not!"

"You brought me to your world and then both of us to mine. That's powerful magic."

"The raven did that, not me."

"She helped. You pulled and she pushed, or maybe the other way round."

No. Aunt Opal was the one who could work magic. Baxter was just an ordinary guy without any special talents, who'd lucked into an extraordinary situation. And an extraordinary lover. But he was too tired to argue, so he simply squeezed back and stared up at the sky.

Midway through the second day, they climbed a gentle hill dotted with strange trees that looked straight out of Dr. Seuss. Baxter expected the Lorax or Horton to make an appearance at any moment, and he was slightly disappointed when that didn't happen.

However, when they reached the crest and looked down into a wide valley, Baxter almost stumbled over his own feet. "Is it some trick of perspective or are those houses tiny?" There were a few dozen round buildings with jaunty cone-shaped roofs, each painted in a different bright and improbable color scheme. His first thought was that they were children's playhouses, but they seemed too small even for that. There were no regular houses for miles around, and cheery little puffs of smoke rose from the chimneys. Also, it looked as if the surrounding fields contained herds of grazing... guinea pigs?

Before Morli could answer, the closest members of their band caught sight of the weird little settlement and grew very excited. "Can we stop, sir?" begged their nearest comrade, one of the hulking Jethros who'd been the first to join. "Please?"

"Not for very long." In response to Morli's reply, a wild cheer arose. Then Morli grinned up at Baxter. "It's Knemibnast."

"What now?"

"Knemibnast. The gnome village."

Baxter should have been past surprise at this point, but he blinked anyway. "Gnomes?"

"Udrodia has the only above-ground gnome settlement in the Ten Kingdoms," Morli said proudly. "I mean, every kingdom has gnomes, but they generally live in caves or underground. Not ours, though. We have Knemibnast."

Baxter had questions—a lot of them—but their followers were hurrying downhill, and Morli and Baxter had to rush if they wanted to stay in the lead. When they grew closer to the houses, Baxter saw that the animals weren't really guinea pigs, although they kind of resembled them. These creatures had long elephant-like trunks and short tusks. "What are those?"

"I'm not sure what they're called in Gnomish, but our word for them is minuscules. The gnomes raise them for milk, meat, and fur. Useful little beasts."

While Baxter was still coming to terms with that, they passed the first gnomes. They were about as tall as his knees and didn't look as he'd expected, based on his world's garden statues. For one thing, both their pants and shirts were made of leather, which reminded him of fetish-wear, and they wore round minuscule-fur hats that resembled Russian ushankas. Their skin was gray, making them look as if they were carved out of stone, but they moved with remarkable speed and animation. And they seemed delighted with their visitors. "Welcome!" they shouted, waving from near their herds of minuscules. Everyone in Morli's gang waved back.

They were greeted at the village by several more gnomes. "Right this way, friends!" said one of them. Baxter wasn't sure of the gnome's gender, assuming gnomes had genders similar to humans. Which was a big assumption.

They were all shaped more or less alike—sturdy and squarish—and none had facial hair. Their voices were all high-pitched, but then, he didn't expect booming words to issue from a two-foot-tall body.

Baxter didn't know where they were being led, but everyone else bounced with excitement as the gnome took them down the village's only street to the tallest round building, sporting chartreuse walls and fuchsia trim. It stood about six feet high, so Baxter probably could have fit inside, but it turned out he didn't have to. The gnome pressed fingers against a black circle painted on the siding, and an entire section of the wall slid aside, revealing the interior. It held wooden shelves filled with pottery cups. Baxter didn't know what he'd expected, but it wasn't this.

Everyone else, though, remained eager. A few at a time approached the opening, gazed around at the cups—no two of which were alike—and then pointed one out. A gnome took a coin from each of them and handed over the cup, which the buyer inspected gleefully, oohing and aahing over the details.

Morli waited until everyone else had made their purchases. "Do you want me to choose one for you?" he asked Baxter.

"Um, sure." Baxter had no idea what was so wonderful about the cups. They were pretty enough, he supposed, but he could have found something just as nice at any arts and crafts fair back home. Still, he smiled when Morli bought him a blue glazed one with a painted castle.

"That's the Udrodian Royal Palace," Morli said. His home, where he might never go again.

"Thank you." Baxter wished he could kiss him. He should have worked out a backstory in which their followers could know they were lovers.

After the gnome closed up the building, Baxter expected that they'd all return to the main road. Instead, the gnome took them further down the village street, past the last of the buildings, to... a well. A fairly ordinary well, as far as Baxter could tell, although sized for gnomes. Morli gestured at their volunteers to go ahead, and then he hung back slightly, waiting with Baxter.

"What's the deal?" Baxter asked.

"The waters of Knemibnast. According to lore, if you drink them, your wishes will be granted."

"*All* your wishes?"

Morli chuckled. "No. Just important ones. You can see how out of the way this place is, but some people travel for days to come here."

"It sounds as if the gnomes created the lore to fleece people out of their money."

"Maybe they did. But people go away happy, so maybe it's worth it. And you get to keep the cup as a souvenir."

Baxter almost rolled his eyes. But then he sank into thought as he watched people drink their mugfuls of water and step back with huge smiles and shining eyes. Even if their wishes didn't come true, they were probably getting their money's worth. His Aunt Opal had collected glass doorknobs, sometimes spending outrageous amounts on essentially useless objects. But when he was a boy, she'd explained that the knobs made her happy, and therefore the money was well spent.

Eventually it was Baxter's turn. Their host dipped Baxter's cup into the bucket and handed it back with a wink. "Best of luck to you," the gnome said, seemingly sincere.

The water tasted awful, bitter and metallic, but Baxter drank it all to avoid offending anyone. Morli downed his in one long swallow, earning applause from his followers.

If Knemibnast had been in Baxter's world, there would have been a souvenir shop before they returned to the road. It would have been filled with T-shirts, fur hats, and plastic cups. He was happy to be spared that travesty. With their spirits even higher than before, the party continued their journey to the tower.

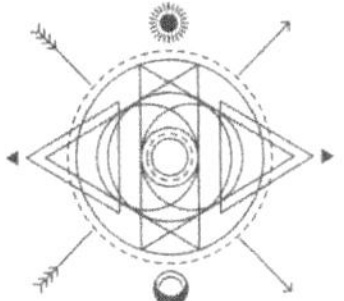

When they reached the Udrodian border, Baxter expressed his disappointment at the absence of dragons.

"We don't have enough to post them everywhere," Morli explained. "They prefer the busier routes, and this one is very slow."

"Don't people come to see the gnomes?"

"Not many. This isn't like Modesto, Baxter. Most people here never leave their home villages."

"Oh, okay."

Morli frowned. Baxter had been so happy during their journey, never complaining, even about the dingiest inns. He hadn't been particularly thrilled with the Aksesh Forest, but Morli couldn't blame him for that. Once they had regular access to good food, Baxter had cheered up and taken a keen interest in Morli's world. He even said he liked the tiny hamlets they passed through, the places so obscure that even most Udrodians had never heard of them. But now he looked sad, and Morli didn't like that at all.

"I'll tell you what. After we rescue the princess, I'll take you to Burslem. The dragon there is especially big and pretty—she has purple and green scales—and she's interesting to talk to. You'll like her. Um, assuming you don't want to return to Modesto right away." Morli knew he was only postponing the inevitable, but even a few more days with Baxter would be precious.

Baxter's smile reappeared. "You wouldn't mind?"

"Of course not. I like her, and I haven't seen her in a few years. She won't recognize me, of course, but that's fine. She'll like you."

"Wow. Meeting a dragon." Baxter slowly shook his head. "Incredible."

They were on their third day with the recruits who, much to Morli's surprise, remained just as cheerful as when they'd left. None of them had ever been outside the kingdom before, and they found it very exciting, even if the other side of the border looked exactly the same. They'd formed friendships and several romances during the journey and enjoyed the spectacle they created as they passed through the villages. Thankfully his promises of adventure hadn't been empty.

And they liked him, even though none of them knew who he was. Baxter called him Modesto, a joke between them that also shared the first two letters of Morli's real name, making slips less likely. As far as the entourage knew, Modesto was a baker who'd been set upon by magic, resulting in his current odd looks and his passion for conquering the tower. Baxter said that this story wasn't really a lie but simply truth-adjacent. Anyway, the troops believed it, and they vied eagerly for their leader's attention. He continued to discuss their families and their lives, and they thrilled at his interest.

Morli had never been popular before. It was an odd feeling.

Now the whole lot of them were traipsing happily through the sliver of Kovell that lay between Udrodia and Vraelum. Soon they'd cross another lonely border, pass through a small forest—much tamer than Aksesh—and reach the tower. Morli's heart raced uncomfortably in anticipation, but he was careful to maintain a positive demeanor.

Ah, but Baxter could tell. He walked close by Morli's side and whispered, "Everything okay?"

"Nerves. I guess I'm not much of a hero."

"You're a man who's willingly returning to the place he died in order to rescue a helpless victim. That sounds like a hero to me."

Morli shot him a grateful glance. "But I'm scared."

"You'd be a fool if you weren't." He must have seen Morli's skeptical look because he chuckled. "What about Frodo? Was he a hero?"

"Of course."

"But he was scared. And reluctant. And tempted by that stupid ring."

Huh. Morli hadn't really thought about it that way. In the hero stories of his world, men and women had marched forward without a single qualm or nervous stomach, tackling danger with as few worries as Baxter tackled Target. But maybe those heroes *had* been scared, and those parts got left out in the retelling. In Morli's opinion, they ought to be left in. Fear made the heroes more human and their feats more wondrous.

He lifted his chin and stepped livelier.

A few miles later, when they were almost to the Vraelum border, Baxter spoke again. "I don't want to freak you out, but do you have a plan?"

"More or less."

"Share?"

"I'm going to have everyone encircle the bramble. Then I'll have everyone attack at once, but without stepping into the vines. They're not trying to reach the tower, you see—they're just, um, distracting the bramble. That way they're not likely to get hurt." He hoped that part proved true. He doubted the bramble could reach out at everyone at once.

"Okay. And then what?"

"I'll step forward and make my way to the tower."

"Like you did last time."

Morli scowled at him. "Last time I was alone. Also, in addition to my sword, we now have your poison. I'll use that as well."

"There's not very much of it. Too bad we couldn't bring a tanker truck of the stuff with us."

Trying to imagine how they would have transported a truck, Morli laughed. "I'll make do with what we have." Then he grew more serious. He'd been needing to tell Baxter something, and there was no better time than now. "Look. If the bramble kills me—"

"Don't!"

"Hush. This is important. If it kills me, encourage the crew to keep at it. But if they become afraid and want to quit, let them. Don't make them feel bad about it." He didn't want to be responsible for a lifetime of guilt for any of these eager young people.

"Fine," Baxter said reluctantly.

"And another thing. I died once already. Everything that's happened since then—most especially my time with you—has been the most precious gift that anyone could ever receive. If I die again, my last thoughts will be how grateful I am to have known you." He paused, held up a hand to stop Baxter from replying, and took a deep breath. "To have *loved* you, Baxter Quirke. Because I do. With all my heart." His voice cracked on the final word, but that was fine.

Although Baxter wasn't crying, his eyes glittered. "Oh God. I love you too. Aunt Opal's spell worked so well. It brought me happiness. It brought me you." And then tears maybe did fall, because he rubbed his forearm across his face.

It wasn't fair that they'd had so little time together, but then, life wasn't fair—not in either of their worlds. And Baxter was right; they'd shared so much happiness. Morli wished they could make love one last time. Maybe he could steal a kiss when they reached the tower.

They all stopped for lunch before leaving Kovell. It was a lovely day to be dining al fresco, with just a tinge of autumn crispness to the air. If Morli had been back at the palace, he would have baked tarts from firefruit, which ripened for only a week or so and only at this time of year. It was a delicate berry, and you had to handle it gently and cook it exactly right, or else you ended up with tasteless mush. But if you were very careful, and if you used the accompanying spices with a practiced hand, firefruit tarts were ethereally glorious, a triumph on the tastebuds. Even the queen had praised his firefruit tarts the previous year, despite her awareness of who had made them.

They all rose, gathered their things, cleaned up their messes, and walked on.

There was no dragon, of course, at the drab little village peopled with sour-faced locals who expected them all to be killed. The villagers probably didn't want Osenne to be rescued, because then they'd lose an important source of revenue.

Baxter must have figured this out. He frowned at a self-important woman who'd apparently appointed herself village leader. "You can still have tourists after the rescue, you know. Just do a package thing. Charge them for room and board here, then take them out to the tower and have a guide tell them all the gruesome stories. Let them inside, even, so they can see where the princess slept. Charge them for souvenir twigs from the bramble."

"A package thing," the woman said, looking thoughtful.

"Sure. You can even have people dress up and role-play —nasty sorcerer, snoring princess, brave rescuing prince. You know, the gnomes are only a day away. You could collaborate with them, maybe. Get people to come to the region for a big holiday. They drink the waters, they tour the tower... maybe you build a couple of really good restaurants or attract some entertainers to put on nightly shows."

Morli smiled to himself as the woman wandered away. She might not follow Baxter's suggestions, but the villagers would certainly have something to talk about for a while.

A short distance past the village, they entered the forest. Centuries earlier, there had been a palace nearby, a summer home for the royal family of Vraelum. These trees had been the royal woods, where the kings and queens and their children and friends went on dignified hunting excursions that were mainly an excuse to show off their riding clothes. While the nobility played, they'd kept troops at a nearby fort, ready to protect them if the need arose. Eventually, for reasons unknown to Morli, Vraelum royalty had abandoned the palace. It had fallen to ruin, the forest had become wilder, and all that remained of the fort was the tower holding Princess Osenne.

A discerning eye could tell that this forest had once been tame. Some trees grew in rows, planted to replace those felled for building material or firewood. The remains of old paths still appeared here and there, as did piles of stone—now overgrown—which had once been pavilions where the hunters took their fancy luncheons. At one point they passed some tree branches that bore faded, tattered remnants of once-bright banners.

It was the kind of place that seemed to swallow noise, as if sounds had been worn away by age and disuse. Due to both the oppressive atmosphere and some trepidation at nearing their destination, the recruits became more subdued. They spoke quietly, if at all. Not a one of them faltered, however; they remained Morli's steadfast followers.

"Look at them," he whispered to Baxter. "They've had adventure, just as I promised. They could turn back right now and arrive home with plenty of stories to keep them popular at the inn. But none of them are doing that."

Baxter shook his head as if Morli were missing something important. "It's because of you. They believe in you."

"But they don't even know that I'm their prince."

"That's irrelevant. Look, you lured them in with a good sales talk. But you've kept them because you're kind and funny. You've learned everyone's name. You ask them about themselves, which makes them feel valued and interesting. You're an excellent leader, and *that's* why they follow you. You don't need titles when people respect you."

Respect. That was something Morli had never aspired to, mostly because he didn't think he'd get it. He'd been tolerated at best. And yet here he was. How had it happened? He looked over at the big, handsome man walking beside him and knew the answer.

"You *are* a sorcerer," he said.

"Not that again. Look, it's cool. I am perfectly satisfied to be your right-hand man. I don't need special powers."

"But you have them." It was hard for Morli to keep his

voice low. "Consider everything that has happened around you. A bucket of sourdough starter and vegetable scraps became a man—with all of a human's feelings and needs and shortcomings. And instead of turning into a horrified mess at being thrust into a strange world, I was fascinated. Charmed, sometimes. Then when I realized I must return home, you made that happen. And once we were here, I found confidence I've never before possessed and talents I didn't know I had. When I faltered, you shored me up. You might not be aware of it, but you've been working your magic all along, and it is *spectacular*."

Baxter was gaping at him. "I... I don't think.... I haven't—"

"You have. Your magic is like yeast. You take the ingredients—the flour, the liquid, the salt—and when you add the yeast, that's when you get bread. Your magic makes things happen. And you know what else? We're going to defeat the tower. How can we not with a powerful sorcerer on our side?" He was absolutely positive of this truth, whether Baxter believed or not. And he was awed as well, because this was powerful sorcery.

"If I'm such a big wizard, how come my life back home kind of sucked?"

"Maybe because you never tried to draw on this talent. Maybe something about your world stifles magic—which would explain why most people don't believe in it. Maybe you work best when acting on others' behalf." Morli shrugged. "I don't know. And it doesn't matter. Look at how much you've achieved already."

Although Baxter was frowning, his eyes carried a certain glint that Morli sensed was the beginning of belief.

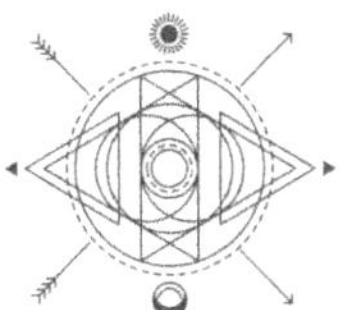

18

The company halted when the tower came into view. Morli didn't blame them. It was one thing to talk about it when you were two kingdoms away, quite another to face it in person. He decided a small pep talk was in order, so he placed himself in the center of the road and began to speak loudly.

"I believe that we are going to rescue Princess Osenne. Every one of you will return home with reward money in your purse, tales to awe the entire town for years, and the sure knowledge that you've done the right thing in saving an innocent young woman. But even if that doesn't come to pass, you are still heroes. You're not royalty or knights—you're ordinary people. And you're doing an extraordinary thing."

He wasn't lying or saying pretty words to get compliance. He liked these people very much, and he admired their willingness to be dragged away from their comfortable lives and put themselves at risk. To demonstrate his respect, he executed his deepest bow.

They cheered for him and for one another, and he

remembered that not so long ago, he wouldn't have been able to persuade these people to go indoors during a rainstorm. But now he could lead them, and he felt comfortable doing so. Thanks to Baxter, who was beaming at him proudly.

Oh, Baxter. Morli would die in that bramble a dozen times more if it meant he'd be granted just a little more time with him. Baxter had continued his stubborn refusal to go home and his insistence on joining the attack. But after this was over, he'd need to return to his regular life in Modesto. Morli's heart tore at the very thought of it.

Now wasn't the time to grieve, however. They had a princess to rescue.

They hurried toward the tower at a rapid clip, no longer chattering. Fists gripped weapons; eyes steeled with resolve.

Morli had hoped to see the raven here. Not that she owed him anything, but he missed her and would have liked to see her once more. He hoped that if he died, she'd be the one to eat his eyes again.

The grassland hadn't changed since his last visit, but this journey was infinitely better. The sun was gentler, and his feet were comfortable in good boots. He was accompanied by sixty strong men and women who were eager to aid his victory. Most importantly, however, Morli had found love—with the most remarkable person he'd ever met.

Perhaps he ought to say something about that before it was too late.

"Baxter?"

Trotting along at Morli's side, Baxter turned his head. "Something wrong?"

"No. Not at all. I just need you to know that I love you."

"What?" Baxter stumbled and would have fallen if Morli hadn't grabbed his arm.

"Love. True love. I've never loved anyone, but I do now. I wish we could spend a lifetime together, but every minute with you has been a gift."

"But I'm just Bax—"

"You're not *just* anything. You're the one and only Baxter Quirke, and I love you."

Baxter was always handsome, but when he smiled like that, he stole Morli's breath away. If Queen Hamnita's enchanted looking glass was intact and here right now, it would proclaim Baxter the fairest in the land—the fairest in *any* land—and it wouldn't be lying.

"I love you too," Baxter said.

It was probably foolish, but Morli *had* to do it. He pulled Baxter close and tugged his head down for a long and breathless kiss. And, oh, it was magical. It made him feel more alive, stronger, and more capable than ever before. It made him feel as if he could fly.

The recruits, who weren't nearly as shocked by this turn of events as Morli expected, clapped and whistled. A lot of them locked lips too, confirming the romances that had bloomed during the journey.

Baxter broke the kiss. His hair was a mess, his face flushed, his lips wet and luscious. And his eyes sparked. "Let's go rescue that princess!" he shouted.

EVEN AS CONFIDENT and eager as everyone felt, it would be stupid to storm the bramble without any organization. So Morli stopped them a stone's throw away and began to pace the perimeter as he strategized. Baxter accompanied him.

The tower looked the same as last time, impenetrable

and fierce, with the remains of previous heroes hanging like grisly ornaments.

"Jesus Christ," Baxter muttered, staring at a skeleton wrapped so completely in vines that it was impossible to tell where the skull was. "How many people have died trying to save this princess?"

"I don't know."

"Is anyone holding the sorcerer responsible?"

Morli shook his head. Sorcerers tended to operate above the law, limited only by their consciences—if they had them —and the threat of other sorcerers. He didn't say this to Baxter, however, lest he once again protest that he couldn't possibly be a sorcerer. Despite all evidence to the contrary.

They had gone around the corner of the tower and were hidden from their followers when Morli came to a halt.

"Something wrong?" Baxter asked.

Morli raised a shaking hand. "That's me."

The body hung perhaps fifteen feet off the ground, pierced in numerous places by vines as thick as a man's forearm. There was nothing left of his skin and flesh, so he wouldn't have recognized himself it weren't for the ridiculous boots his parents had made him wear. One had fallen off his corpse and disappeared, along with the foot, but the other remained.

It was a very odd sensation to stand there, breathing, feeling his heart beat, looking into his own empty eye sockets. He wasn't even sure how to react. It didn't seem quite right to mourn.

Baxter put his arm around Morli's shoulders. "I can't begin to imagine the pain you experienced." His voice sounded choked.

"It... hurt. But the worst part was dying alone."

"That won't happen again."

"Baxter—"

"I mean it. I sincerely hope we all survive, but in any case, I'm not leaving your side today."

Oh, demons' doorknobs. "But I don't want you to die."

"I don't want that either. So let's make sure we don't."

As soon as those words left Baxter's mouth, a tingle ran down Morli's spine, making him gasp. Baxter must have felt it too: he yelped and hopped back. "What the hell was that?"

"Magic."

Baxter whirled around in a circle. "Is the sorcerer here?"

Morli didn't know whether to laugh or strangle him. "A sorcerer is here, yes. *You* are. That was your magic. I'm sure of it."

"I…. But I didn't *do* anything."

"You said you'd make sure we survive."

"But…." Baxter made an exasperated noise. "Okay, let's say I *am* Mr. Wizardpants. Fine. Now what? Do we just go marching in and expect those thorns to stay out of our way? 'Cause I don't want to test that." He cast a significant glance at Morli's corpse.

"Nor do I," Morli admitted. But without knowing what Baxter's magic was capable of, it was hard to know how to act. He stared at the vines, remembering with far too much clarity what it felt like as they pierced him. "If you could consciously control your magic, what would you do?"

"I'd say abracadabra and make the entire bramble disappear."

"Is that a spell?"

Baxter sighed. "No. Not really. It's just something that stage magicians say before pulling a rabbit out of a hat. I don't know why."

Morli had no idea why anyone would want to pull a rabbit out of a hat. It seemed like a very strange thing to do.

And would the rabbit be relieved or would it object? Maybe rabbits in Baxter's world liked hats. There were so many mysteries about that place.

"Well," Morli said after shaking his head to clear it, "the bramble hasn't disappeared. So consider the tools at your disposal and think what you could do with them."

"The tools." Baxter got that thoughtful expression, which was promising. He removed his dagger from its sheath, looked at it for a moment, and then returned it. He shrugged off the backpack—which, as Morli's employee, he'd insisted on carrying—and pulled out a few items of clothing and the remains of their lunch. They'd bought the bread at the border village, and although it had been entirely mediocre even when fresh, it wasn't worth using as a weapon.

But then Baxter held up the plastic bottle he'd brought from home. "This. I'd use this."

"Your weed killer?"

"Yeah. I'd make it strong enough to kill instantly instead of making the plant slowly wither. None of us want to sit around here for weeks."

Suddenly excited, Morli clapped his hands. "Yes! I was going to have our people distract it with their weapons while I tried to get to the tower. But what if they use your poison instead? And I'll use the poison to clear my path."

Baxter shook the bottle. "There's only a few ounces left. That would kill a dandelion, I guess, but not that monster." He waved at the bramble.

"If you can make it stronger, you can make it *more*." That was obvious.

Baxter opened his mouth as if to argue, then closed it again. He tucked everything but the bottle back into the pack and reshouldered it. "Whatever. This is silly, though."

Morli put his hands on his hips and decided to resort to his strongest weapon. "What would your Aunt Opal say right now?"

"That's a low blow."

Morli simply raised his eyebrows and waited.

After a moment of glaring, Baxter sighed. "She'd say to stop being so negative and to believe in myself." He quoted her in a high, sing-songy voice: "'You can't have a positive outcome without positive ambitions.'"

"I agree with Aunt Opal," Morli said. And then he had an idea. "How about if I offer extra incentive for positive ambitions?"

"Not dying isn't a good enough incentive?"

"It's a start." Holding up one finger for each point, he continued, "Not dying. Getting to meet a dragon. So much lovemaking that when you get home you won't walk right for a week."

Despite his clear efforts to suppress it, a wide smile spread across Baxter's face. "That's pretty good."

"I think so too. Now come on."

THEIR LITTLE ARMY seemed relieved when Morli and Baxter reappeared. Morli didn't know if their followers had thought them dead or assumed they'd run off. He and Baxter trotted over to them, Baxter still clutching the bottle.

"Listen carefully," Morli said to the crowd. "Put down your bags and remove any flappy clothing. You don't want anything loose getting caught in the vines. Have your weapons at hand and the cups you bought in Knemibnast." They looked at one another in confusion but obeyed.

Morli nodded his approval. "You're going to be stationed

at intervals around the bramble. There are enough of us that we should be relatively close to each other. When I tell you to, you'll attack. Your goal is simply to kill the vines. Meanwhile, Baxter and I will be making our way to the tower." Even if this worked, he wasn't sure how they'd get into the tower. But one problem at a time.

"Sir?" called a gangly man named Ghaf. "How will we kill the vines?" He held a pair of tailor shears that were probably perfect for cutting cloth but would find even the thinnest vine shoots a challenge.

Morli grinned savagely. "With poison! Magic poison!"

That earned him impressed whistles. Udrodians had a healthy appreciation for poisons, perhaps because that was how an unsettling number of Morli's forebears had met their ends. Not to mention the ones who'd been put into enchanted sleeps, like Osenne, or turned into horrible beasts, or otherwise suffered unhappy consequences.

"Are you ready?" Morli asked. He heard calls of agreement, but they weren't enthusiastic enough. He needed his warriors almost in a frenzy. So he employed a technique he'd seen in one of the movies Baxter had showed him. "I can't hear you. I said, are you ready?" This time the shouts were louder. He shook his head. "Come on. You're *heroes*! Are. You. Ready?"

This time the roar was so loud that the citizens back in Udrodia might have heard.

At Morli's command, the recruits ran to the tower and spaced themselves along the bramble so that, with outstretched arms, they could nearly touch hands. Good. Then Morli turned to Baxter. "Time for magic, Mr. Wizardpants."

He saw Baxter take a few deep breaths, square his shoulders, march to the closest person, and fill her mug with the poison. Then the next person's. And the next. His pinched expression made him look as if he expected something horrible to happen at any moment. But once he filled the cup of the fourth person, he began to relax. Even more so by the fifth, then the sixth.... By the tenth he was smiling so broadly that the top of his head could have fallen off.

He worked the complete circuit and the bottle never emptied. "There's even more!" he said to Morli.

"I told you."

"How about we assess how strong it is before we head in."

Morli nodded. Then, in a voice that he hoped carried all around the tower, he yelled, "Splash the bramble!"

Every member of his army dashed the contents of their mug onto the plant.

For a long and awful minute, nothing happened. Then a terrible sound split the air, an inhuman shriek that made Morli want to cover his ears. And the bramble began to wither. The leaves on the outermost vines began to turn brown and curl at the edges, falling to dust and leaving the vines bare. The woody parts slumped toward the tower, revealing hard bare earth beneath. Corpses fell to the ground with rattles and thuds.

But then the plant's retreat slowed. A few slender shoots began to unfurl.

"More!" Baxter shouted. He ran the circuit again, refilling cups, and then again and again, until he was gasping for breath and the bramble was reduced to a thin, swaying layer of vines close against the tower walls.

Morli stopped him before he could run around again. He wasn't sure Baxter would make it. "Give me the bottle, please."

Baxter didn't have enough oxygen to argue, but he

looked unhappy as he handed it over. He stuck close to Morli, who drew his sword with his dominant hand and marched ahead.

The last time he'd done this, he died.

But last time he was alone. Now Baxter was here, and Baxter loved him.

Morli lifted his sword and charged. He sloshed the poison ahead of him as he went, requiring a good bit of coordination, but he managed. He couldn't spare a glance at Baxter, although Morli heard him panting close by.

The remaining bramble cowered under the onslaught, pressing back more and more tightly. Apparently in desperation, it thrust a few vines forward, but Morli danced out of their way. As, he hoped, did Baxter.

The bramble had finally diminished enough to expose the stone wall. There was no door in sight. Morli moved several steps clockwise and pushed forward again. Still no door. Again. Nothing. Again. Baxter kept up with him, and they both hacked at the reaching tendrils. Members of their army helped as best they could, but few of them possessed weapons that allowed them to attack without endangering themselves, and Morli kept shouting at the rest to jump back.

It was like a nightmare. Morli and Baxter kept circling but met nothing but bramble and stone. The vines would not die back completely. In fact, as Morli's arm grew heavy and his lungs felt tight, the bramble seemed to rebound, sending vines forward with increased energy and frequency. Morli tripped over a corpse—his own, for all he knew—and a vine twined around his leg at once, making him scream with pain as it dragged him inward. But Baxter yelled too and slashed at the vine until it released.

Morli scrambled back to his feet. He felt blood pooling

in his boot, hot and sticky. But he limped onward anyway and for a moment felt renewed optimism—until the bottle of poison emptied.

"Sorry!" Baxter gasped. "Can't. No more."

Morli tossed the bottle at the bramble; it bounced back with a useless little clunk. As if realizing what that meant, the plant shook and stirred. New leaves began to sprout, thorns grew bigger and sharper, tendrils reached forward with increased ferocity. One swiped across his face, digging in with its thorn and nearly blinding him. Another wrapped around his left arm. He was able to hack at that one with his sword, but before the vegetation fell away, it stripped off a good deal of Morli's flesh.

He could barely raise his sword any longer. Everything hurt. Breathing was agony. And still the bramble gained ground, with no tower door in sight. A woman shrieked in pain, and Morli knew what he had to do.

"Fall back!" he screamed through his fading energy. "Everyone fall back!" He couldn't turn to see if they obeyed. A fleeting glance, however, told him that Baxter remained. He was bleeding.

"Fall back," Morli begged him.

Baxter simply growled in response.

The bramble was filling in. Surrounding them. Soon Baxter would be entirely cut off from escape. Couldn't he see that? Before Morli could warn him, a tendril wrapped around the ankle of his wounded leg. He kicked it away, ducked to avoid another, and hopped away from a third. His leg gave and he almost fell. As he scrambled for balance, a thick vine ensnared his right arm, piercing and squeezing with such strength that he couldn't even scream. He dropped the sword.

Morli collapsed to his knees. He didn't make a sound as

a vine burrowed into his belly. All of this was so familiar...
and yet not. He didn't want to die, and surely it would be
final this time. He wanted Princess Osenne to be freed. And
gods above, he wanted Baxter to live. But Baxter had made
his own decisions, as had Morli, and at least they were dying
together. Their corpses would hang in the bramble, side by
side.

"Love," he mouthed, but no sound came out. He was
sure Baxter knew anyway.

Something fluttered to the ground in front of him. His
waning mind thought at first that it was a yellow leaf, but
no. Too large. Too angular.

Oh. An envelope. Thank the gods, Baxter was using the
feather to send himself home.

Morli felt another tingle along his spine, similar to the
one before but much stronger. It might have hurt if he
weren't already in agony. A split second later, a boom like a
thousand thunderclaps rent the air. His ears still echoed
with it when the stones crashed and the bramble suddenly
released him.

Morli fell face forward into blackness.

19

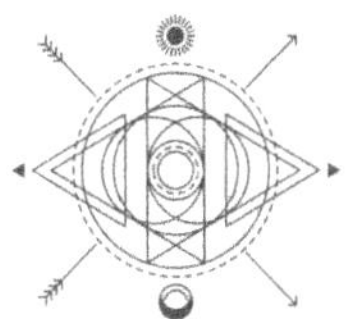

Feathers brushed his face.

"You can have my eyes again," he rasped.

"I'd rather not, but thanks."

That wasn't the raven.

With some difficulty Morli blinked his lids open and discovered Baxter gazing down at him, gently dabbing Morli's cheek with a soft cloth. They were still outside the tower, Morli's head pillowed in Baxter's lap and about sixty concerned faces gathered around, staring at him.

"What?" That was all Morli could manage, which he thought was rather a lot under the circumstances.

"Why didn't you tell us he was a sorcerer?" said a woman in the crowd. "It would've been nice to know."

Baxter answered for him. "I didn't know myself until today. Not really."

There was some back-and-forth after that, mostly having to do with how someone could have all those magical powers and not bloody know it. But Morli didn't care about that. He licked his lips and attempted an entire sentence. "What happened?" There. Only two words, but it counted.

Baxter dabbed at him again. "The, um, bramble sort of went poof."

"Poof?"

"It's gone."

Morli tried to turn his head to look, but there were too many people in the way. And then he realized that although he was lightheaded, he wasn't actually in pain. He looked down at himself: flesh covered in dried blood but intact. Holes in his clothing but not in himself. He struggled to a sitting position. "I'm not dead."

"Your sorcerer did that too," called the woman.

Morli looked at Baxter. "Oh?"

Baxter was blushing. "I, uh.... It was awful. You were...." He squeezed his eyes closed for a moment. "There was so much blood. I don't even know what I did, exactly. It was so fast. I just sort of wished...."

"Wished that I'd live."

"Yes."

Morli threw himself at Baxter with enough force that they nearly toppled over. Sometimes words just didn't suffice, so he gave Baxter a kiss that expressed all of his gratitude, pride, joy, and love. It was a long kiss that nearly suffocated them both. The crowd clapped when they were done.

Laughing, Morli leapt to his feet and gave Baxter a hand up. He felt *wonderful*. Strong and healthy and full of energy. Until he remembered the envelope and the realization hit. "Oh no!" He clutched Baxter's arm.

"What? What is it? Are you okay?"

"The feather. You used the last feather."

"Yeah, and it worked really well."

Morli shook his head impatiently. "How will you get home?"

"That really wasn't my biggest worry at that moment." And in fact, Baxter seemed perfectly calm about it, as if he got trapped in other worlds all the time. Probably the import of what had happened hadn't yet sunk in.

"But you can't—"

"Let's talk about it later. You have a princess to save. Everybody's insisting we go in first."

Right. The princess. "You found the door?"

Baxter scratched his head. "Um, not exactly." He waved a hand awkwardly, and the crowd parted, giving Morli a full view of the tower. Or what was left of it. Because what had once been a solid stone wall now had a gaping hole, three times as wide and twice as tall as a door. Chunks of rubble lay on the bare ground among scattered desiccated corpses. There was absolutely no sign of the bramble.

"Poof?" Morli said, voice shaking a bit.

"Those feathers are amazing. If I ever have the chance to write a Yelp review for Marden's Magic Emporium, they're getting five stars."

Morli didn't know what Baxter was talking about, but that was nothing new. What was important now was that it looked as if access to Princess Osenne was unimpeded. "We should go inside."

By mutual accord, Morli went first, sword drawn, stepping over the threshold with care. He hadn't heard tales of further dangers inside the tower, but that didn't mean there weren't any. Maybe the nasty sorcerer just hadn't mentioned them to anyone. Baxter was right behind him, dagger in hand and probably wishing he had additional feathers.

There had been some discussion about how many—and exactly who—would enter. It seemed awkward to have sixty people crowding in, yet nobody wanted to be left out. Finally, Baxter chose ten people through a magical ritual he called "rock, paper, scissors." Everyone else had to remain outside for the time being, with the promise that they could explore the tower later.

The structure had been built for practical purposes, not beauty or luxury. The ground floor consisted of a single large, high-ceilinged room. The remains of wooden shelving lay in heaps near the walls, along with a few scraps of what might have been leather, a thick layer of dust, and lots of dead mice and spiders. Back when the tower had been part of a fortress, this room was probably the armory, although no weapons remained.

"Cheery place," Baxter muttered.

"Could use a bit of decoration."

Baxter shot him a grin. "It has a great open floor plan, but it doesn't tick all my boxes." Another of his mysterious statements.

The narrow stone stairway required them to climb single file. It hugged the wall, seeming to curve endlessly up, with steps worn in the middle by countless feet. At least there was illumination via a central shaft that carried columns of sunlight from windows high above.

They finally reached the next story. Morli and Baxter gave it a quick look, but it contained nothing but rotting bed linens, heaps of broken furniture, and even more dead spiders and mice. They continued up.

"How did the sorcerer get the princess here anyway?" Baxter asked. "Did she drag her here and then enchant her?"

"No, the princess fell into her sleep in the palace in the capital."

"Then how did she get here?"

Morli thought for a moment. "I have no idea."

"You'd think that would be a standard part of the story. I

mean, did the sorcerer haul the princess over her shoulder and carry her? Were horses involved? More magic? And how the hell did she get her up all of these stairs? Did she have accomplices?"

Morli turned to grin at Baxter over his shoulder. "I love you."

The next floor was even emptier than the last, without even a decent selection of small dead things, and the same with the next floor. Morli was beginning to wonder if they'd never reach the princess. Maybe endless stairs were part of the enchantment. But Baxter seemed pretty cheerful and kept up a running commentary. "Anyone who lived in this place wouldn't need a StairMaster, that's for sure. And they better not have issues with vertigo or their vestibular system."

"Have you noticed that this stairway is backward?"

Baxter was silent for a moment. "Backward?"

"Usually they're clockwise. They provide better defense that way."

"Huh. So why's this one counterclockwise?"

"I have no idea."

"You guys need to step up your storytelling. You have plot holes."

Morli snorted at him, turned another curve, and came to a wooden door blocking their way. It looked very solid and was certain to be bolted from the inside. Yet when he gave a tentative push, it swung open with a creak.

And there they were.

This room at the top of the tower was surrounded by windows and bathed in light. The vaulted ceiling soared far overhead. The painted patterns on the floor tiles had long since worn away, and the wall-hung tapestries had faded to almost indistinguishable blurs. In the center of the room was a carved stone bed, and lying there on her back was Princess Osenne. Or so Morli presumed.

He and Baxter stepped cautiously forward, their ten recruits a slight distance behind.

The princess was a sturdy girl who looked as if she would excel at sports. Contrary to what the tales said, she wasn't especially beautiful, although she had a pleasant face. She wore riding clothes—but no boots—and her chest rose and fell slowly. There was nothing troubled in her expression; she simply looked fast asleep.

"How long has she been like this?" Baxter whispered.

"Almost twenty years." Morli had whispered too, which was silly since the point was to wake her up. He went on in a normal voice. "I remember hearing about it when it happened, but I was pretty young."

"At least she hasn't aged. Although I bet it's going to suck that all her friends have grown up and gone on with their lives. Married, kids...."

"She's a princess. Members of royalty have very few friends."

Baxter gave him a sympathetic look. "Sometimes all you need is one or two very good ones. Okay. How do we wake her up?"

"The stories say with a kiss."

But Morli didn't move forward, and Baxter frowned. "That's kind of... gross. She can't consent to it."

Morli had selfishly been thinking of himself and how he didn't want to kiss anyone but Baxter. But Baxter had an excellent point. Poor Osenne had been victimized enough already; forcing her to receive a kiss from a stranger was added cruelty. "I agree." He looked at his followers, and they nodded too.

Maybe he could wake her up in the usual way. He stood

beside her stone bed, cleared his throat, and said quite loudly, "Princess! It's time to get up." She didn't stir. Then he touched her very gently on the shoulder, and when that didn't work, more firmly. Nothing. Her breaths continued to come slow and deep, and her eyelids never fluttered.

As uncomfortable as the idea made him, maybe a kiss was the only option. They couldn't leave her here to languish, and unlike the sorcerer, they had no way to transport her back to her family at the palace, at least five days away.

He was mulling over the options when he noticed movement in his peripheral vision. He turned to see a large black bird settling on the windowsill. "Raven!" Morli hurried over and opened the glass. The raven greeted him with a friendly croak and flapped into the room, startling everyone but Morli and Baxter. And Osenne, of course. After a few circuits, the bird landed beside the princess's head.

"Hey, don't eat her eyes," Baxter said. "She's still alive."

The raven gave him a reproving look before giving her wing a quick preen. She then hopped onto Morli's shoulder, which made the troops gasp. Morli hadn't expected it either, but he didn't mind, not even when she played with his hair. "Are you thinking your nest would look nice with some green strands in it?"

She made a sound that seemed suspiciously like a laugh. And then, although Morli might have imagined it, one of the princess's eyes twitched. "Raven," he said, almost too excited to speak, "could you please, um, sing as loud as you can?"

The raven laughed again—probably knowing that nobody admired her kind for their singing—and then she let out a squawk loud enough to make Morli's ears ring. This time the princess's eyelids definitely moved, although they didn't open.

"Raven, do you have friends and family you could gather quickly? If you help us wake the princess, I can promise all of you a share in the reward. Whatever you like."

She cocked her head and then flapped to Baxter's shoulder, where she bent her head and mouthed at a large brass button at the neck of his tunic. "Shiny stuff?" Baxter said. "Would you like shiny stuff? Buttons and, um, beads and...."

Morli interrupted. "Wake the princess and I'll take you to a market, where you can pick out as many shiny trinkets as I can afford." It seemed only fair.

She clacked her beak twice, dipped her head, and flew off through the open window.

"Was that more sorcery?" asked a man named Frexin. Morli liked him. Frexin had spent the entire journey gushing at length about even the most pedestrian things he saw—"Ooh! Did you see that haystack? It was so big!"—and flirting with a man named Qagabo. For his part, Qagabo was agreeable but slightly dense, and didn't yet seem to realize that Frexin was flirting. Morli had thought more than once about intervening.

"That wasn't me," Baxter answered. "She's just a bird. But I've heard ravens are really smart. And I don't know about here, but where I come from they have a reputation for being tricksters." He added more quietly, "Or symbols of death."

Frexin, who either didn't hear the last part or ignored it, bounced on the balls of his feet. "That's so interesting! I like to feed the pigeons sometimes at home. They're not very smart, I don't think, but they have pretty colors. I like watching them. Are there pigeons where you come from?"

Baxter smiled at him. "There are. And some people feed

them there too."

That seemed to delight Frexin, who was easier to please than anyone Morli had ever met. He launched into an enthusiastic monologue about all the creatures he fed back home—apparently a horde of strays relied on him—and how he planned to use some of his reward money to buy them better rations. Some of the other people rolled their eyes, but with an air that said they were used to Frexin and rather fond of him.

Just when Morli was starting to worry about the ravens, a raucous chorus slowly increased in volume. He and Baxter hurried to open more windows, and a few seconds later a flurry of black feathery creatures came hurtling into the tower. There might have been a hundred or more, although it was impossible to count. They landed on windowsills, the floor, and the stone bed. Some landed on people's shoulders, making their perches startle and then laugh. The raven he now thought of as his returned to his shoulder. And then she called, a shrill sound that echoed from the ceiling and walls.

A moment later, they *all* called.

It was the most incredible din anyone could possibly imagine, so strident and sharp and complex that Morli couldn't breathe. It was as if the noise took up all of the space and air in the room, and even all of the light. It was hard to remember that anything but the noise had ever existed.

Then the birds fell silent, leaving the humans gasping and shocked.

The odd thing was that there were no aftereffects, no ringing in the ears or temporary deafness. Just an ordinary, expectant silence... until the princess slowly sat up, yawned, and stretched.

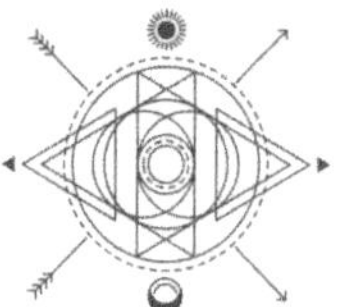

20

Morli hadn't given any thought as to what would happen after the princess was rescued. Baxter kept sighing over that and muttering about plot holes, although Morli pointed out that Baxter himself hadn't planned for it either.

Luckily, Princess Osenne was happy to do all the planning, once her situation had been explained to her. "I am *so* going to have a conversation with that sorcerer," she said, flinty-eyed. Morli almost felt sorry for the sorcerer.

Osenne pulled Morli and Baxter aside. "All right. I bet my parents promised my hand in marriage to whoever rescued me. I think either of you could claim me, so who's it going to be?" She looked resigned and not remotely enthusiastic.

Morli smiled at her. "With all due respect, Your Highness, Baxter and I would rather have each other. And we both agree that you should choose your own spouse, assuming you want one at all."

She grinned and gave them both hugs. "I am so glad to hear that! And I'll make sure you get a huge reward."

Osenne ended up spending a day of celebration on the grass outside the tower with Morli, Baxter, and the troops. There was singing and dancing and telling exaggerated versions of exploits. Even the ravens joined in with shows of stunning aerial acrobatics. Everyone had a wonderful time, and when night arrived, they all slept under the stars.

In the morning, Osenne took charge. She chose three volunteers to accompany her to the palace. One of them was a young woman she'd spent a lot of time dancing with the day before, so maybe a marriage might happen after all. "Now here's what we're going to do," she announced to the rest of them. "You don't have enough supplies to wait for the reward. So most of you are going home. But—" She turned to Morli. "Is there a village nearby?"

"It's a couple hours away."

"Good. Two of you will stay in the village. I'll make sure they know my family is paying the costs. The two will wait there until your compatriots arrive back with your reward, which you'll carry back home to share with the others."

She didn't ask whether they agreed with the plan—she was royalty, after all—but in any case, nobody seemed to have objections. While the troops gathered to decide who would stay, she drew Morli and Baxter aside. "What are your plans?"

They looked at each other hopelessly. They hadn't had time to discuss that, and Morli suddenly remembered that Baxter was stuck. "We haven't decided yet," he said.

"You can come back with me! I can promise you good positions in the palace. We could always use more heroes and sorcerers—the good kind, I mean."

She seemed genuinely enthusiastic about her offer, and something inside of Morli clicked into place. Not because he especially wanted to work for the Vraelum royal family, but because she wanted him to. She valued him—just as Baxter did, although in a different way. These two fine people found him worthy, which must mean that he was.

He gave her a warm smile. "Thank you for the offer. It's very kind. But I think... I'd like to go home."

"I know the feeling," she said with a nod.

"Baxter?" Morli asked.

"I'd like to see your home."

Morli very nearly started crying again.

MORLI AND BAXTER took a room at the village's only inn, and the brothers that Baxter insisted on calling Jethro took another. The villagers treated all of them like royalty, which the brothers enjoyed, Baxter tolerated, and Morli endured. He and Baxter spent a lot of time strolling through the countryside, talking about nothing of consequence.

One afternoon nearly a week after the rescue, they sat on a fallen log along the bank of a busy little stream, watching leaves float by. They'd made love in a nearby meadow, but hurriedly, because the days had turned a little too chilly for bare skin. Baxter sighed and leaned against him. "You smell so good. You always smell so good."

"Is that why you like me?"

"I love you. And no, but it's a nice bonus." He put his arm around Morli and kissed the side of his head.

Morli took a deep breath. "Baxter, we need to—"

"Oh no. Don't say it. I hate that phrase."

"But we do. We can't keep avoiding it."

"Why not?" Baxter removed his arm and sighed, his shoulders slumping. "Ugh. I hate this talk."

"We can find another sorcerer," Morli said firmly. "A really powerful one, but a good one. One who, um...."

"Knows what the hell he's doing?"

"Yes. And they can find a way to send you home. I'm sure of it." He *was* sure of it. If magic had transported him to Modesto and brought both of them back here, it could surely send Baxter home. Morli wished that weren't true, and then he felt horribly guilty for wishing it.

"Home." Baxter sounded hollow. Then he squirmed around to face Morli. "Tell me the truth. Absolute honesty or I'll... I'll turn you into a frog. Do you want me to go?"

"No," Morli replied in a whisper, not meeting his eyes. "I'm sorry to be so selfish, but I don't want to lose you."

"Ever? As in, do you want to be stuck with me forever after?"

"More than anything."

Baxter's smile sprouted and grew broad, his eyes like warm honey. "Good. I'd like that too."

It was hard to speak when your heart was trying to beat its way out of your chest. "B-but your home...."

"My home." Baxter made a dismissive gesture. "What do I have there that's worth more than you? Nobody will miss me. My boss can find someone else to deal with Mr. Saucy."

"But everything in Modesto is so... sophisticated. Your computer and television and telephone and car. We don't have those things."

"No, and you also don't have toxic air. I'm not gonna lie —I've missed plumbing, and I bet when winter rolls around I'll turn nostalgic for central heat." Baxter cradled Morli's face in his palms. "But here I have you, and nothing in my world can top that."

Of course they kissed. And then they made love again on the pebbly bank of the stream, and neither of them minded the chill. In fact, Morli thought he might never feel cold again. Not with Baxter at his side.

They walked slowly back toward the little village, holding hands. A large black bird circled high above them. "What do you want to do when we leave here?" Baxter asked. "'Cause I'm game for whatever makes you happy."

"We have to take the ravens to the market, and I promised you a dragon."

"That you did. Then we play it by ear? Or do you have a plan?"

Morli hesitated. He did have an idea, one he'd been sitting on for days, but he wasn't sure whether he was brave enough for the revelation. Then he remembered that he'd battled the bramble twice, so of course he was brave enough. He took a deep breath. "A bakery?"

Baxter didn't scoff or laugh or dismiss the notion. In fact, he smiled encouragingly. "Yeah? Tell me more."

"If our portion of the reward is enough, I'd like to go back to my home city and open a bakery. I'd make and sell breads, and some pastries too, I think. I would introduce Udrodia to pizza."

"Do I get to assist you and take care of advertising?"

"Please." In barely a whisper.

Baxter tugged him to a halt just long enough to seal the deal with a kiss.

EPILOGUE

Baxter watched as Morli slid the fragrant brown loaves out of the oven, setting them aside before putting new ones in. All of the morning's earlier breads had sold, and a few customers hovered outside The Raven's Feather, waiting for the new loaves to cool. He had a final batch rising, a recipe made from some rare grains a trader had brought the previous month. Baxter considered that recipe his favorite. Then again, he tended to say that about all his breads—and he meant it.

Once the final loaves were baking, Morli would start a large batch of pizza dough. Baxter would make the sauce and grate cheese, and the pies would be ready by dinner-time. They'd proven to be so popular that three other bakeries were producing their own copies. Morli and Baxter didn't mind. Imitation was flattering, and their own shop couldn't possibly keep up with demand. Besides, everyone knew their pizza was the best. And as the signs outside the shop proclaimed, The Raven's Feather was the *original* home of Udrodian pizza. They were nice signs; Baxter had spent a long time painting them.

Morli brushed loose flour from his hands and nodded at Baxter, reminding him to turn his attention back to the display counter, where a matronly woman had finally made her choice. "Four of those, please," she said, pointing at the catberry muffins.

"I think you'll really enjoy these, madam. They're not quite as sweet or indulgent as cakes, and some of the ingredients are healthful. But they're also delicious."

She fluttered her eyelashes at Baxter. "I'm sure they're delightful." She leaned forward slightly and lowered her voice as if sharing a secret. "I've heard that Princess Osenne and her wife come all the way from Vraelum just for your muffins!"

"They have been our guests, yes."

In truth, she'd only come once. It was a long journey, and eight months after her rescue, she still had many matters to take care of at home. Also, she liked the muffins well enough, but her real favorites were Morli's sourdough bread and chocolate chip cookies, another of Baxter's introductions to this world.

But he knew the woman wouldn't care about any of that. She handed Baxter some coins, took her packet of muffins, and vowed to return the next day to try something else. Then she sailed away.

Baxter rearranged a display of cupcakes, which sent his mind to pleasantly naughty places. Thanks to the tattoo on Morli's lovely ass, Baxter was never going to feel neutral about cupcakes again.

Morli came over and stood close, leaning against him. As always, his wonderful scent eclipsed even the baking bread. He had a dusting of flour in his hair and a bit on his nose, and he radiated serene joy. Baxter felt the same way—

happier than he would have thought possible, Aunt Opal's spell magnified a hundredfold. He loved helping Morli and tending to customers, and although he missed a few of Modesto's twenty-first-century comforts, he'd gained infinitely more than he'd lost.

He'd been cautiously practicing a little sorcery, trying out some very modest and tentative spells, and the results were promising. Morli often acquired small burns—a hazard of spending a lot of time sticking his arms into ovens—and now Baxter could heal them. All it took was a bit of concentration and singing a stanza of Harry Nilsson's coconut song, which seemed to work well as an incantation. Maybe someday he'd be confident enough to help the sick and wounded. But for now, he was utterly content to be a fledgling mage and baker's assistant.

"You know what tomorrow is?" Morli asked.

"Fiveday?" Udrodians had a complicated calendar, with weeks that sometimes varied in length and months that just plain confused Baxter. It had something to do with the double moons, apparently, which was all well and good but left Baxter in a constant state of disorientation about the day. Then again, the pandemic had pretty much accomplished the same thing back home, so he was used to it.

"Yes, Fiveday. Do you have plans?"

That was the day they kept The Raven's Feather closed so they could get some rest and catch up on other projects. Their building—with the bakery downstairs and their private rooms up—was comfortable but old, so things tended to need repairs. And usually they'd spend a little time at The Drunken Ogre, a very pleasant pub just down the street. Baxter had been urging customers to take their pizzas over there because The Drunken Ogre had the best ale in the neighborhood. As a result, business was booming at the pub, and the landlords gave Morli and Baxter free drinks.

Fiveday was also when they did their shopping, often stopping by a certain market stall to buy shiny little baubles for their raven. She would croak her approval and carry the trinkets to her nest on the roof, which Baxter imagined must look completely bedazzled by now. She often had her bird friends over for visits, maybe so she could show off her bling, and her parties tended to get noisy. But Baxter had endured far worse neighbors than that.

He turned his attention to Morli's question. "I was thinking of drawing up a flyer for the hand tarts." These were a brand-new item, inspired largely by a certain brand of toaster pastries that were, of course, unavailable here. As were toasters, in fact. But Baxter intended to market these to busy people who worked long hours and might appreciate a tasty snack that was easy to carry, store, and eat. First he had to come up with a clever name for them, and then maybe a character to go with. *Not* Mr. Tarty, though. That just didn't work.

"You could do that," Morli purred. "Or we could stay in bed all day, reading and... entertaining ourselves."

"Oh? And how might we do that?" Baxter waggled his eyebrows.

"Well, there was that thing we tried the other night...."

Baxter was going to inquire as to which particular thing Morli had in mind, but there was a sudden disturbance outside, which sent the bread-awaiting customers scrambling to the other side of the road, gaping and wide-eyed. A moment later, two men in gaudy uniforms swept into the shop with capes swirling, gold trim glinting, and scabbards shiny enough to blind.

Morli went very still.

The uniformed men scanned the shop as if expecting a cadre of trolls to launch a surprise attack. When all they saw were items appropriate to a bakery, one of them turned to Morli and Baxter and cleared his throat. "Her Majesty, Queen Gafrooz of Udrodia, and His Royal Highness, Prince Algar."

Oh, shit. Baxter sensed this wouldn't be good.

The queen marched in first, resplendent in a many-layered dress that mimicked a bright wedding cake. Her blonde hair was arranged in ornate curls, and a fortune in jewels hung from her neck and adorned her fingers. She had a narrow face with thin lips and cold eyes; apparently that obvious wealth hadn't made her happy. Her son was a younger, sneerier version of her, the kind of man who, as a child, likely bullied anyone smaller than him. Neither of them resembled Morli at all, but then, the current Morli looked nothing like the original. Both members of the royal family were a little out of breath, probably from walking up the steep hill from the palace.

An uncomfortable silence fell; the queen seemed to be waiting for something. The uniformed pair stood back, near the door, while curious faces crowded the windows and peered inside. Baxter had met royalty only twice before, and in both cases the royals in question were unconscious; he didn't know what to do when royalty was wide awake. At long last Morli gave a small bow—nothing like the deep, graceful ones Baxter had seen him execute—and Baxter awkwardly copied him.

"Welcome, Your Majesty and Your Highness," Morli said, a slight waver in his voice. "We're honored by your presence."

The queen sniffed disdainfully, as if she'd expected

more. Then she looked at the displays of muffins, cookies, and small cakes. There wasn't much inventory this late in the day, but Baxter always made sure it looked attractive and tempting. The prince wasn't interested in the pastries. He was too busy admiring his reflection in a glass case.

"I have heard," began Queen Gafrooz, "that The Raven's Feather is enjoying a certain popularity among my people."

Morli was still stiff but managed an answer. "Thank you, ma'am. We're honored that our fame has reached you."

"I've also heard that Princess Osenne of Vraelum sampled your wares during her visit to my kingdom."

"Yes, ma'am."

Algar made a rude noise. "It's only because of the rumors, Mother. That they were there when she got out of that stupid tower. And that they have trained birds. All a lot of nonsense and no substance."

Baxter had previously wanted to punch Algar, knowing how he had treated Morli in the past, but now the urge was so strong that his hands ached. If he hadn't been afraid of taking a first step down the path of evil sorcerery, Baxter might have tried to throw a small curse at him. Nothing huge like sleeping for years. Just... really bad breath. Jock itch. Repeated ant invasions in his bed. Farting during solemn occasions.

Perhaps sensing Baxter's feelings, Morli placed a gentling hand on his arm while addressing his brother. "Sir, you're welcome to sample our wares and judge for yourself."

Algar opened his mouth, likely ready with a taunt, but the queen shut him up with a glare. "We shall taste what you have to offer," she announced.

Morli gave another bow. "Of course."

They didn't have any servingware in the shop, so Morli

grabbed two clean mixing bowls. Then he took his time cutting small pieces of everything in stock. He even cut a pair of slices from the loaf that had been intended for their dinner that night. While he worked, Queen Gafrooz stood in various careful poses as if someone were painting her, while Algar mostly scowled. Maybe he couldn't help it. Maybe one day his face really *had* frozen like that, and now he was eternally stuck looking like a disgruntled weasel. Neither the queen nor the prince paid Baxter any attention at all, which was fine with him.

Somehow Morli had composed himself, and by the time he set the bowls onto the counter, he looked tranquil and confident. "Please help yourselves," he said.

The royals were visibly displeased with the presentation, but with a put-upon expression, the queen took a morsel of muffin and popped it into her mouth. Algar followed suit. They tried to keep their expressions disdainful, but Baxter saw the surprise in their eyes, and so did Morli, who smiled. "That's one of our unique specialties. If you like something sweeter, may I suggest the cookie?" He pointed.

They liked that a lot, especially Algar, who looked tempted to lick a bit of soft chocolate from his fingers when he was done. And they didn't complain about the tarts or the cakes or the honeyfruit bars. They ate every crumb.

They saved the bread for last, which was backward but not Baxter's problem. And when the Queen took a bite—the slice still slightly warm from the oven—her eyes widened. "Oh!"

"Is everything all right, Your Majesty?" Morli asked.

"This is...." For a brief moment, she looked sad. Then she cleared her throat. "This is very good."

"Thank you, ma'am."

"I haven't had bread of this quality since my son— Since last autumn."

Next to her, Algar, still chewing, flashed a nasty little smile but said nothing.

Morli bowed more deeply this time. "We do our best to produce high-quality baked goods. We believe it's an honorable business."

"Quite. You should be very proud."

"Thank you." Morli didn't cry, but on his behalf, Baxter felt close to tears.

Queen Gafrooz straightened her back. "I should like to invite you to become the royal bakers. You shall live in the palace, where you will be given every luxury and high salaries besides, and you shall bake bread and sweets such as these for the royal table."

Morli's smile broadened and he tipped his head slightly. "Thank you, ma'am. That is very generous of you. But Baxter and I will remain here at The Raven's Feather."

If the queen seemed shocked at the refusal, Algar was apoplectic. "Do you know what a privilege you're being given, you idiot? Most people would give anything for such distinction!"

"I'm sure that's true. Nevertheless, Baxter and I will remain here."

"How can you be so obtuse! We're talking about the royal palace."

"Of course. I'm sure it's delightful." Morli shrugged. "But I think of myself as an artist, and an artist needs the appropriate atmosphere in which to work. I'm afraid the palace will stifle me. We'll stay here. However, if you send a messenger, we'll make sure to have loaves and pastries for you daily."

Algar's face had gone satisfyingly purple. He clearly wasn't used to not getting his way, and it appeared as if, at any moment, he might throw himself to the floor, kicking and screaming. But the queen gave Morli a long, considering look. Finally she nodded. "Very well. But we shall expect our bread every day."

"With great pleasure, ma'am. And there will be no charge, of course. Consider it our contribution to our king and queen."

She almost smiled at that.

The queen and prince left the shop—Algar still looking like a sulky child—and the uniformed men followed. Baxter hurried over and locked the door, then gave the waiting customers a "just a minute" gesture through the window. He didn't want an audience, so he took Morli's hand and towed him back to the storeroom.

"Wow," Baxter said.

"Yes."

"I used to hate being an only child, but maybe it's not so bad after all."

Morli grinned. "He's awful, isn't he?"

"And he's going to be king someday?"

"Theoretically. But Tassos, the next older brother? He's been coveting the crown his whole life, and he'd do better. And Algar's allergic to shellfish." Morli's green eyes momentarily gleamed.

Baxter wasn't sure of the significance of that but decided it didn't matter. "They didn't recognize you."

"No."

"Are you okay with that?" He searched Morli's eyes but found no sorrow.

"Very much. Prince Morli is dead. Long live Modesto the

baker. I'll send them bread and have the satisfaction of knowing they enjoy it. And I have you and the bakery and... all my dreams have come true. It's so much better being a happy baker and a beloved partner than a miserable prince."

Baxter knew exactly what he meant. He pulled Morli into an embrace and nuzzled at his neck, thinking himself the luckiest man in two worlds. God, he was so grateful to Aunt Opal, and the raven, and the vampire at Marden's Magic Emporium. He was so happy to be exactly where he was.

"That sorcerer was right," Baxter pointed out. "The one who said you'd rise above the king and queen."

Morli opened his mouth as if to argue, but when the meaning of the pun hit him, he laughed instead. "I guess so. I have dough rising every day."

"And your man rising every night."

That led to kissing and groping that would have gone on much longer, except it was time to take the bread from the oven. But Baxter caught Morli's arm before he could return to the shop front. "You know, we have this great concept back where I come from. Not too many people achieve it, but I think you and I can."

"Another baked good?"

"Something even better than that."

Morli pretended to scoff. "What's better than baked goods?"

"Happily ever after, my love."

"That sounds like an excellent concept." Morli took Baxter's hands in his. "Wish for it, sorcerer."

What the hell—it was worth a shot. Baxter closed his eyes, took a deep breath, and flexed an imaginary magical muscle. "I'd like for us to have a happily ever after, please."

A powerful electric thrill ran down his spine and, apparently, Morli's, making them both gasp and jump. But they remained holding hands, both of them smiling so wide it almost hurt. Morli stood on tiptoes to give him a quick kiss, then tugged him toward the front. "Let's go make some dough, Baxter."

RECIPES

These are recipes that my family and I enjoy—and that I can picture Morli and Baxter making. Even the queen would approve.

Because I think of baking as a personal process, I've left all of these in the words of their original creators.

BEST ZUCCHINI SOURDOUGH BREAD

This recipe is courtesy of Emilie Raffa at The Clever Carrot, shared with permission. Make sure to check out her other recipes and her sourdough cookbook too!

For a non-sourdough version, see the recipe notes.

Although this recipe is for bread, you could easily adapt it to muffins by lining a muffin tin with appropriate cupcake liners and adjusting the baking time.

Ingredients
    Butter, for coating the pan
    220 g (2 cups) grated zucchini, from appx. 1 medium zucchini
    125 g banana **weighed with the skin on** (about 1 small banana)
    225 g (1 1/4 cups lightly packed) light or dark brown sugar
    1½ tsp pure vanilla extract
    2 large eggs

100 g (appx. 1/2 cup) sourdough discard OR bubbly, active 100% hydration starter

250g (2 cups) all-purpose flour

1 tsp cinnamon

1/8 tsp nutmeg

1½ tsp baking soda

1/4 tsp fine sea salt

125 ml (½ cup) neutral flavored oil like sunflower (mild olive oil works, too)

60 ml (1/4 cup) milk or unsweetened almond milk

Instructions

How to Prepare your Sourdough Starter: if using left-over sourdough discard, make sure it's in good condition (no brown liquid, no vinegary smell, not straight from the fridge). I use recently fed or just collapsed starter. Alternatively, if using active starter, you'll need to feed it prior to making the recipe and wait for it to become bubbly and double in size.

Preheat the oven to 360 F. Lightly coat (2 or 3) 7 x 3 x 2 mini loaf pans or (1) 9 x 5-inch loaf pan with butter. Note: Using 2 mini loaf pans instead of 3 will you get you slightly taller loaves.

Using a box grater, grate the zucchini on an angle on the side with largest holes. No need to drain out the excess water. Set aside.

Add the banana, sugar, and vanilla to a large mixing bowl. Cream with a hand held mixer or stand mixer fitted with the paddle attachment, about 30 seconds to 1 minute (some small lumps of banana are okay).

Add the eggs, one at a time until fully incorporated. Add the sourdough starter.

Sift the flour, cinnamon, nutmeg, baking soda, and salt together in a separate bowl. Working in batches, add this to the banana mixture.

Add the oil and milk and mix until just combined. Do not over do it; the bread will be tough. The texture should be thick and pourable, but not runny. Add more flour if needed. Fold in the grated zucchini.

Pour the batter into the prepared pan(s). For 2 mini loaf pans, fill about 3/4's full. For 3 mini loaf pans, fill about 2/3's full (these loaves will not be as high). Place onto a baking sheet and transfer to the oven.

Bake for 40-45 minutes for the 2 mini loaf pans (about 30-35 minutes if using 3 mini pans) or 60-65 minutes or more for the standard 9 x 5-inch pan. Cover with foil if the loaf browns too quickly.

Cool in the pan for 20 minutes, and then transfer to a wire rack to cool completely.

Notes

To Store: Wrap the loaves (plastic or reusable wrap) and keep at room temperature. Because of the moisture in the zucchini, the texture will get softer and softer each day.

To Freeze: Once completely cool, wrap the loaves, label and date; they will keep for up to 3 months. Defrost at room temperature.

To Double: Simply double the ingredients as listed. I recommend using a stand mixer.

Non-Sourdough Version: Just leave it out. No additional adjustments needed.

Dairy Free: Use unsweetened almond milk or another plant milk of your choice. Use oil or plant butter to coat the pans.

Gluten Free: Use King Arthur Measure for Measure Flour & a GF sourdough starter

Pan Sizes: (2 or 3) mini 7 x 3 x 2- inch OR (1) standard 9 x 5-inch

BRIAN'S DETROIT STYLE PIZZA

This recipe appears courtesy of my friend and pizza guru, Brian. It makes the best homemade pizza I've ever had, and it's also really easy to do. I make this often enough that I've invested in a Detroit pan, but if you don't have a 10x14 pan, you can use two 8x8 pans.

3 cups (360 grams) of bread flour (I like King Arthur)
 1 cup + 1 Tablespoon (244 grams) of water
 2 teaspoons (10 grams) of salt (1 Tablespoon if using kosher)
 A big pinch of yeast (1/8–1/4 teaspoon)

The night before, mix all the above with a spoon or your hands until you get a shaggy ball. Dump it on the counter and roughly shape it into a ball (don't bother kneading it for more than 30 seconds - if it isn't balled up by then, it won't matter).

Put oil into a bowl or container that is big enough for twice the size of the dough ball. Put the dough ball inside, flip it to get oil on both sides and cover (with plastic wrap or a lid). Leave it on the counter overnight.

The next morning, just fold the dough over on itself a few times and flip it over. Re-cover and leave it until three hours before dinner. (If you don't feel like making pizza tonight, pop it in the fridge at this point – the dough will actually get better each day for up to 5 days. Pull it out of the fridge the morning of your pizza night.)

Three hours before dinner, put a good amount of olive oil in a cake pan (10x14) and put the dough inside. Press the dough out toward the corners – if it shrinks back, cover and let rest for 15 minutes before stretching again. Repeat if needed.

Once the dough is mostly to the corners, cover and let rest for two hours. If you have a pizza or baking stone, pre-heat your oven and baking stone to 450° 1 hour before baking, otherwise, 30 minutes will do.

Make sure the pan edges are well oiled and then pop the dough in the oven for 7-8 minutes or until lightly golden brown. Remove from the oven and let rest for 15-30 minutes. Top with 12 ounces of cheese (a blend of cheddar and Monterey Jack is nice and approximates brick cheese) making sure to get plenty around the edges, and pop back into the oven for 10 minutes. Top with a simple tomato sauce (crushed tomatoes, basil, salt and pepper - you can use that raw, or you can sauté a little garlic in olive oil and cook the sauce for no more than 10 minutes).

If you want to add veggies or meat, place on top of the cheese before the second bake.

BERNICE'S APPLE CRISP

6 apples (pippins are real good)
    ½ C sugar
    ½ tsp cinnamon
    2 tsp lemon juice

Peel and core apples (slice into bowl of water to keep from turning brown). Mix sugar & cinn., lemon juice, and put over drained apples that have been put into buttered baking dish. Then mix

½ C sugar
    ¾ C flour
    1/8 tsp salt
    6 Tbsp butter
    ¼ C chopped nuts (optional)

Mix this until crumbly and sprinkle over apples.

Bake 350F for 45 min.

This makes a small amt. It can be doubled as it is very good.

LINDA'S ONION BREAD

We bake multiple batches of this bread (as rolls) for Thanksgiving—it makes the absolute best turkey sandwiches. But it's also delicious with just butter.

2 Tbsp instant yeast (or 1 Tbsp SAF yeast)
    ½ C warm water
    2 C warm milk
    2 Tbsp butter, melted
    2 Tbsp sugar
    2 tsp salt
    1 tsp celery salt
    ½ tsp sage
    ~6 C white flour
    4 Tbsp instant minced onions
    4 Tbsp water

Rehydrate onions in the 4 Tbsp water and set aside. Put warm water, milk, and butter in bowl of stand mixer. Add onions. Add sugar, salt, celery salt, and sage. Add 4 ½ C flour. Add yeast. Knead. Slowly add more flour (~1/2 C at a time) until dough is cohesive and cleans the sides of the bowl. Let rise in a bowl 30 minutes. Shape into 2 loaves or into balls for rolls. Let rise 30 minutes. Bake at 375F for ~45 mins for loaves, ~20 minutes for rolls. Watch them.

ROSE'S RICE PUDDING

Rice pudding is one of my favorite comfort foods, and with the OJ and almond extract, this one is a little unusual. It's delicious either warm or cold. This recipe comes from one of my grandmothers, and by "glass" she meant one measuring cup.

1 glass raw rice
   3 eggs
   1 tsp vanilla
   ½ glass sugar
   1 Tbsp vegetable shortening
   1 tsp almond extract
   7/8 glass orange juice
   1 glass raisins
   cinnamon

Cook rice. To the warm rice, add all other ingredients except cinnamon. Mix. Put in greased pan. Sprinkle cinnamon on top. Bake at 325F for about 40 mins.

ANN'S KNISHES

My grandmother used to make zillions of these. She'd shape hers by rolling each filled knish into a log, then into a spiral, but you can make them round like dumplings or square if you'd rather. For a truly decadent experience, eat them warm with sour cream on top.

2 C Bisquick
    1 scant C sour cream

Mix well. Let stand at room temp for 1 hr or so.

Take a small piece, mix with all purpose flour. Roll out very thin. Brush with butter.

1 lb dry curd cottage cheese
    1 egg
    salt
    sugar to taste
    a little flour

Mix filling ingredients. Drop small amount on each knish and shape.

Bake on greased pan at 350F for about 15-20 mins.

LINDA'S SUNFLOWER SEED COOKIES

I call these crack cookies because they are seriously addictive. If you want, you can tell yourself that they're healthy due to the oats and seeds. It's a good excuse to eat more.

1 C butter

    1 C brown sugar

    1 C granulated sugar

    2 eggs

    1 tsp vanilla

    1 ½ C unsifted flour

    ¾ tsp salt

    1 tsp baking soda

    3 C quick cooking rolled oats

    1 C shelled sunflower seeds

Thoroughly cream together butter and sugars. Add eggs & vanilla & beat to blend well. Add flour, salt, baking soda, & oats. Mix thoroughly. Gently blend in sunflower seeds. Form into long rolls about 1.5" in diameter. Wrap in wax paper and chill. Slice ½ inch thick. Bake at 350F for about 10 mins or until lightly browned.

Makes ~9 dozen cookies.

Lauren's Italian Herb and Garlic Bread (2 loaf yield)

This delicious recipe is courtesy of Lauren Weidner.

Ingredients:
  4 ½ teaspoons (or two packets) of rapid rise yeast
  2 ½ cups warm water
  1 tablespoon salt
  1 tablespoon olive oil
  7 cups all-purpose flour
  1 tablespoon chopped garlic
  1 tablespoon Italian herb mix
  Corn meal or flour for baking pan

Place warm water and yeast in mixing bowl and allow to proof (3-4 minutes).

Add flour and salt, then add in oil, garlic, and Italian herb mix. Knead by hand until dough springs back immediately when lightly pressed and doesn't tear when you pull it, or knead with the dough hook of a stand mixer for approximately 4 minutes.

Place bread in a greased bowl and allow to double in size. Punch down, then divide into two parts.

Roll out each dough ball out into a rectangle using a rolling pin, then roll up along the long side of the rectangle to create a skinny loaf. Place on a baking pan that's been lined with foil or parchment paper and sprinkled with cornmeal/flour with the seam side down. Allow to rise until double in size.

Create diagonal slices across the top of each loaf (approximately 4 slices per loaf) with a sharp knife.

Bake at 450 ° F for 20 minutes then check for doneness (205 ° F) or sounds hollow when you tap the bottom and has a golden color. Cook for up to an additional five minutes until done. Allow to cool before slicing.

BERNICE'S LITTLE MONSTERS COOKIES

1 C brown sugar

1 C white sugar

3 eggs

1 Tbsp corn syrup

1 1/3 C peanut butter

2 tsp baking soda

½ C margarine (room temp)

1 tsp vanilla

4 ½ C oatmeal (whole)

1 C nuts

6 oz chocolate morsels

1 C of any ONE: dates, raisins, M&Ms plain, or coconut

Put sugars in very large mixing bowl, beat in eggs one at a time. Beat in vanilla, soda, corn syrup. Mix well. Blend in peanut butter and margarine. Stir in oatmeal 1 C at a time. Add chips, nuts, etc. Stir until well mixed. Drop by spoonfuls on lightly greased cookie sheets. Leave about 1 ½ or 2 inches between cookies. Bake 335F for 8 mins, turning sheets around halfway through baking. Makes 8 dozen. Let cool then store.

The Muffin Man by Kim Fielding—*February 4, 2021*
Hexes and Horns by Rowan McAllister—*February 11, 2021*
Must Love Demons by Meghan Maslow—*February 18, 2021*
Elven Duty by Rhys Lawless—*March 4, 2021*
The Young Man's Guide to Love and Loyalty by Clara Merrick—*March 11, 2021*
Geoffrey the Very Strange by Angel Martinez—*March 18, 2021*
Purgatory Playhouse by E.J. Russell—*March 25, 2021*
Stop Dragon My Heart Around by Ari McKay & Rachel Langella—*April 1, 2021*
Haven by Morgan Brice—*April 8, 2021*

ABOUT THE AUTHOR

Kim Fielding is very pleased every time someone calls her eclectic. A Lambda Award finalist and two-time Foreword INDIE finalist, she has migrated back and forth across the western two-thirds of the United States and currently lives in California, where she long ago ran out of bookshelf space. She's a university professor who dreams of being able to travel and write full time. She also dreams of having two daughters who fully appreciate her, a husband who isn't obsessed with football, and a house that cleans itself. Some dreams are more easily obtained than others.

Kim can be found on her blog: http://kfieldingwrites.com/
Facebook: https://www.facebook.com/KFieldingWrites
and Twitter: @KFieldingWrites
Her e-mail is kim@kfieldingwrites.com